D1508293

The Urbana Free Library

To renew: call 217-367-4057
or go to "*urbanafreelibrary.org*"
and select "Renew/Request Items"

SUPERMAN® FAMILY ADVENTURES™

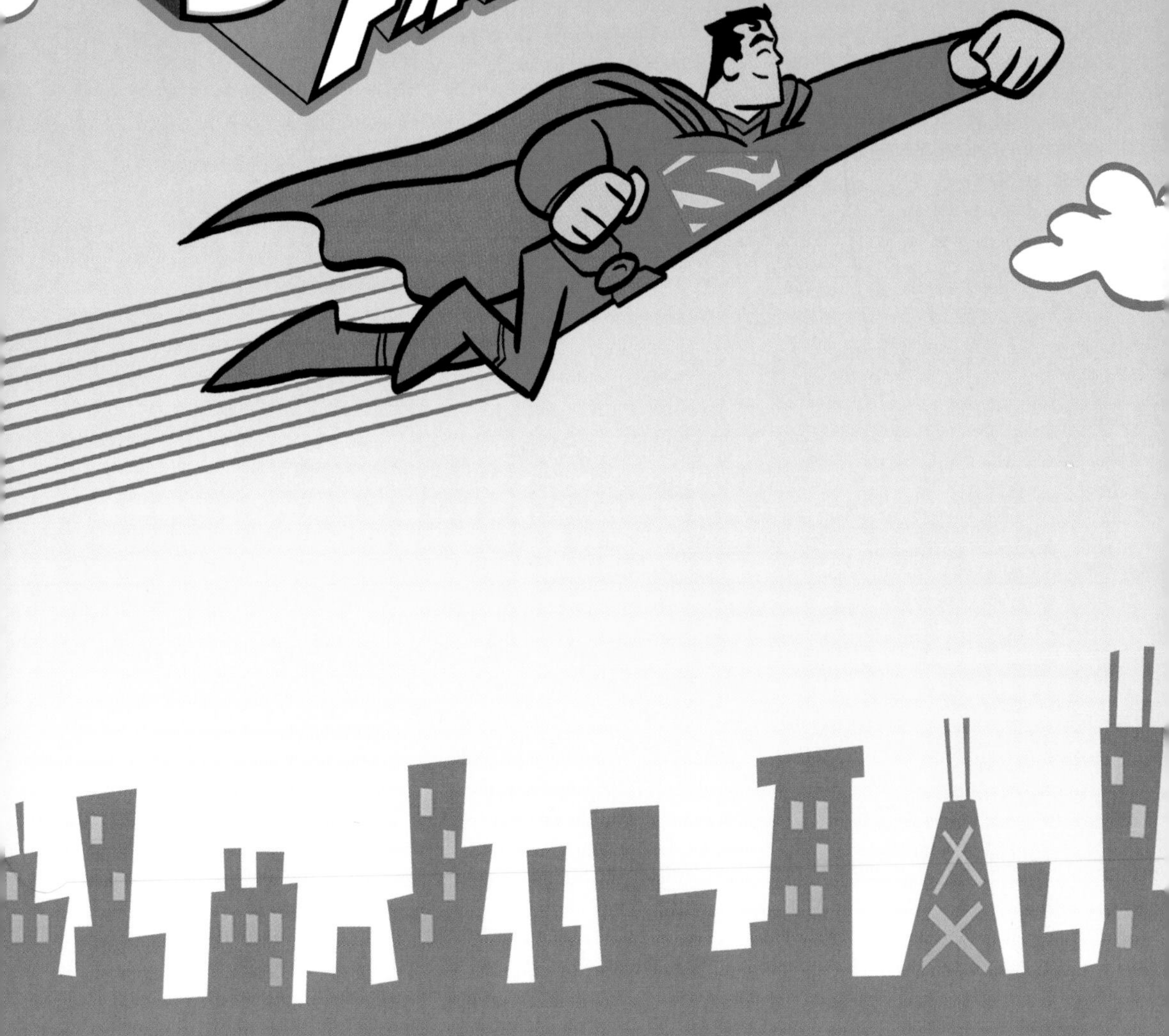

STONE ARCH BOOKS
a capstone imprint

STONE ARCH BOOKS™

Published in 2013
A Capstone Imprint
1710 Roe Crest Drive
North Mankato, MN 56003
www.capstonepub.com

Originally published by DC Comics in the U.S. in single
magazine form as SUPERMAN FAMILY ADVENTURES #4.
Copyright © 2013 DC Comics. All Rights Reserved.

DC Comics
1700 Broadway, New York, NY 10019
A Warner Bros. Entertainment Company

Cataloging-in-Publication Data is available at the
Library of Congress website:
ISBN: 978-1-4342-4791-9 (library binding)

Summary: The City of Metropolis runs into Monkey Mayhem when
Beppo's friend goes crazy! Meet the gigantically giant, ginormously
angry ape TITANO! Can the Super Family make things right? What's
Kryptonite have to do with this? And where the heck is the Chief's
coffee?

STONE ARCH BOOKS
Ashley C. Andersen Zantop Publisher
Michael Dahl Editorial Director
Donald Lemke Editor
Brann Garvey Designer
Kathy McColley Production Specialist

DC COMICS
Kristy Quinn Original U.S. Editor

Printed in China by Nordica.
0413/CA21300442
032013 007226NORDF13

SUPERMAN® FAMILY ADVENTURES™

MONKEY METROPOLIS!

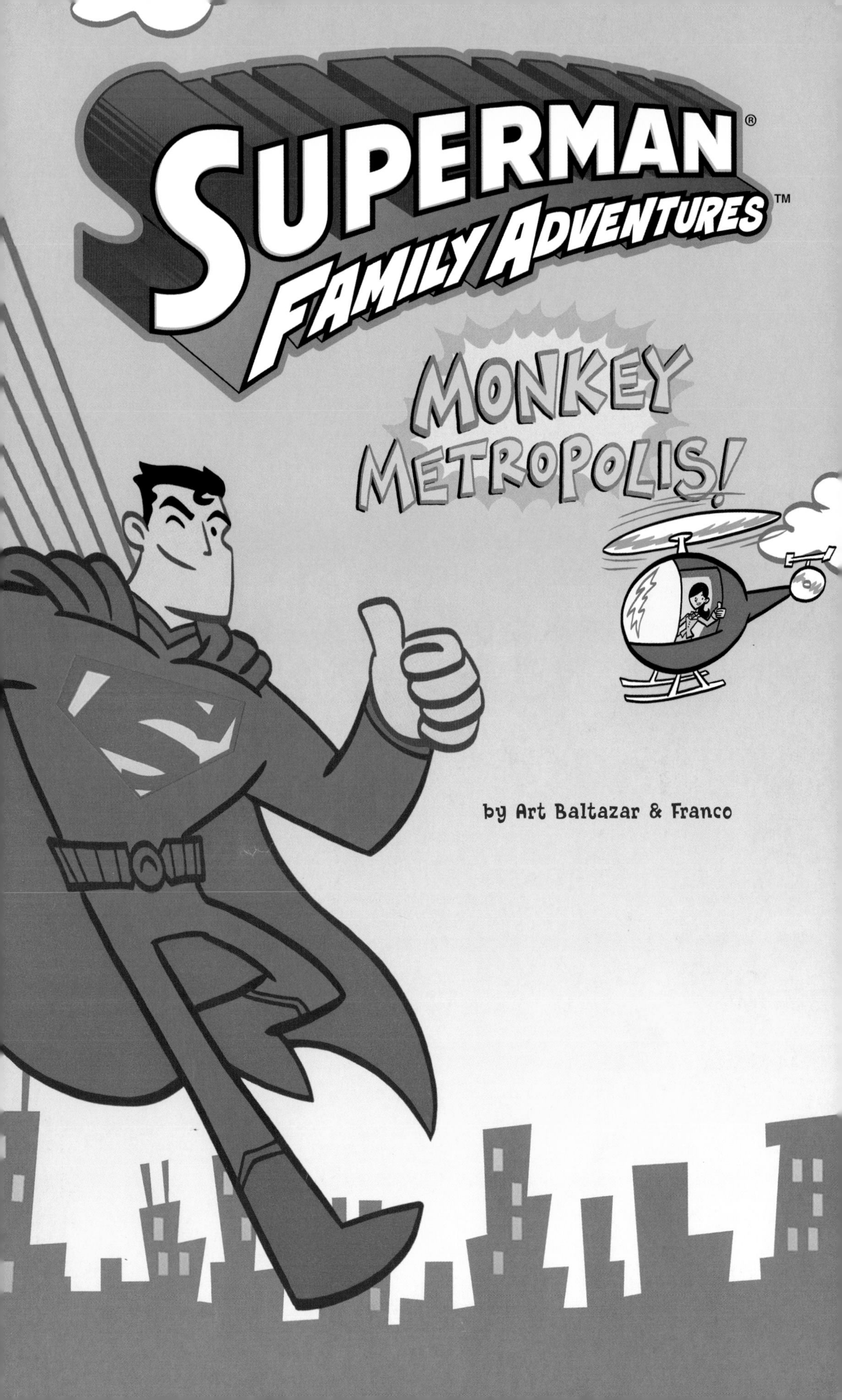

by Art Baltazar & Franco

SUPERMAN®
FAMILY ADVENTURES™

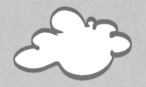

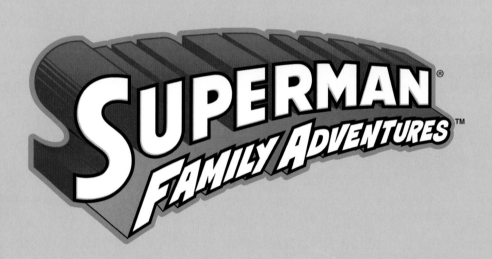

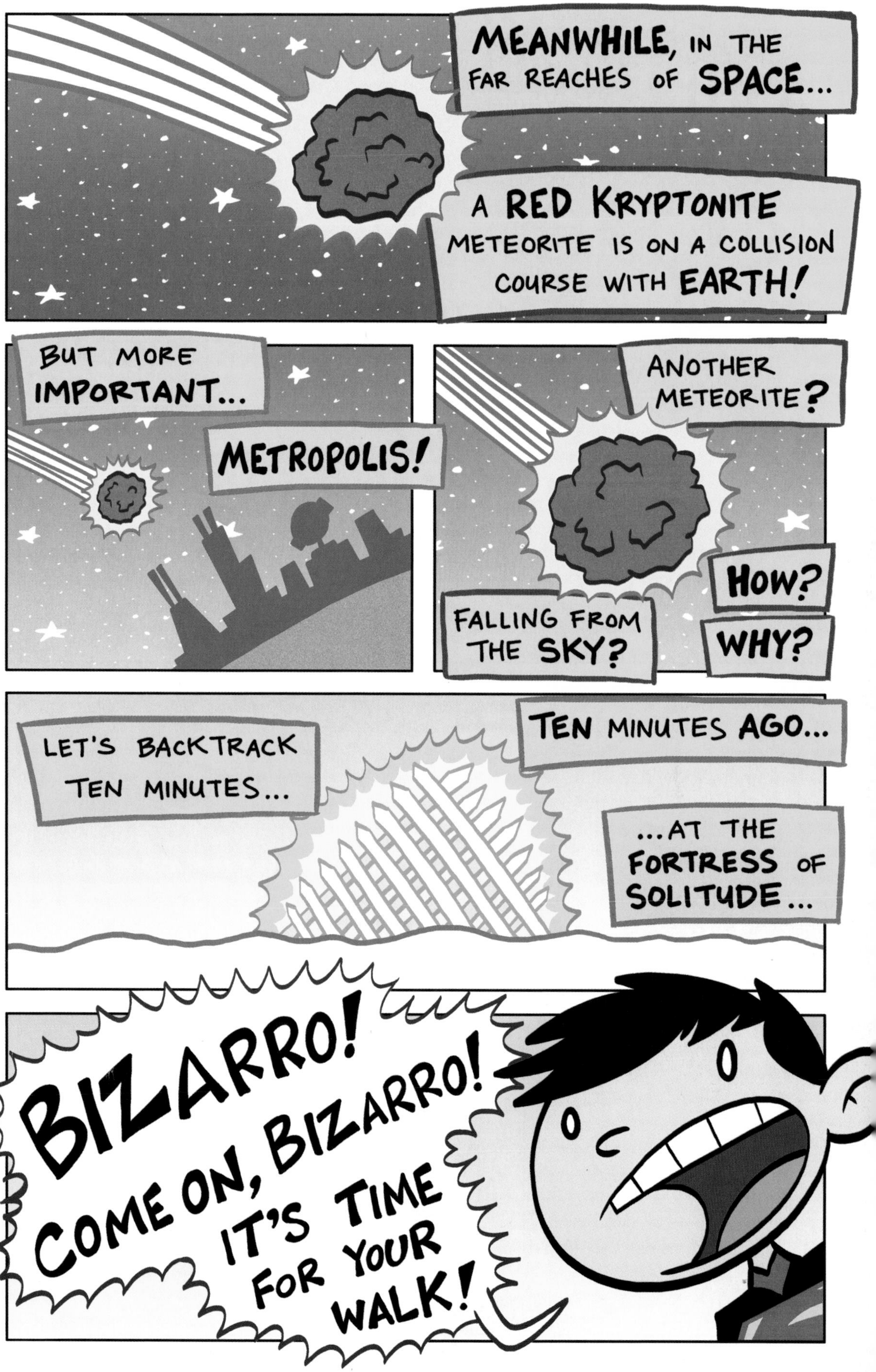
MEANWHILE, IN THE FAR REACHES OF SPACE...
A RED KRYPTONITE METEORITE IS ON A COLLISION COURSE WITH EARTH!
BUT MORE IMPORTANT...
METROPOLIS!
ANOTHER METEORITE?
FALLING FROM THE SKY?
HOW?
WHY?
LET'S BACKTRACK TEN MINUTES...
TEN MINUTES AGO...
...AT THE FORTRESS OF SOLITUDE...
BIZARRO!
COME ON, BIZARRO!
IT'S TIME FOR YOUR WALK!

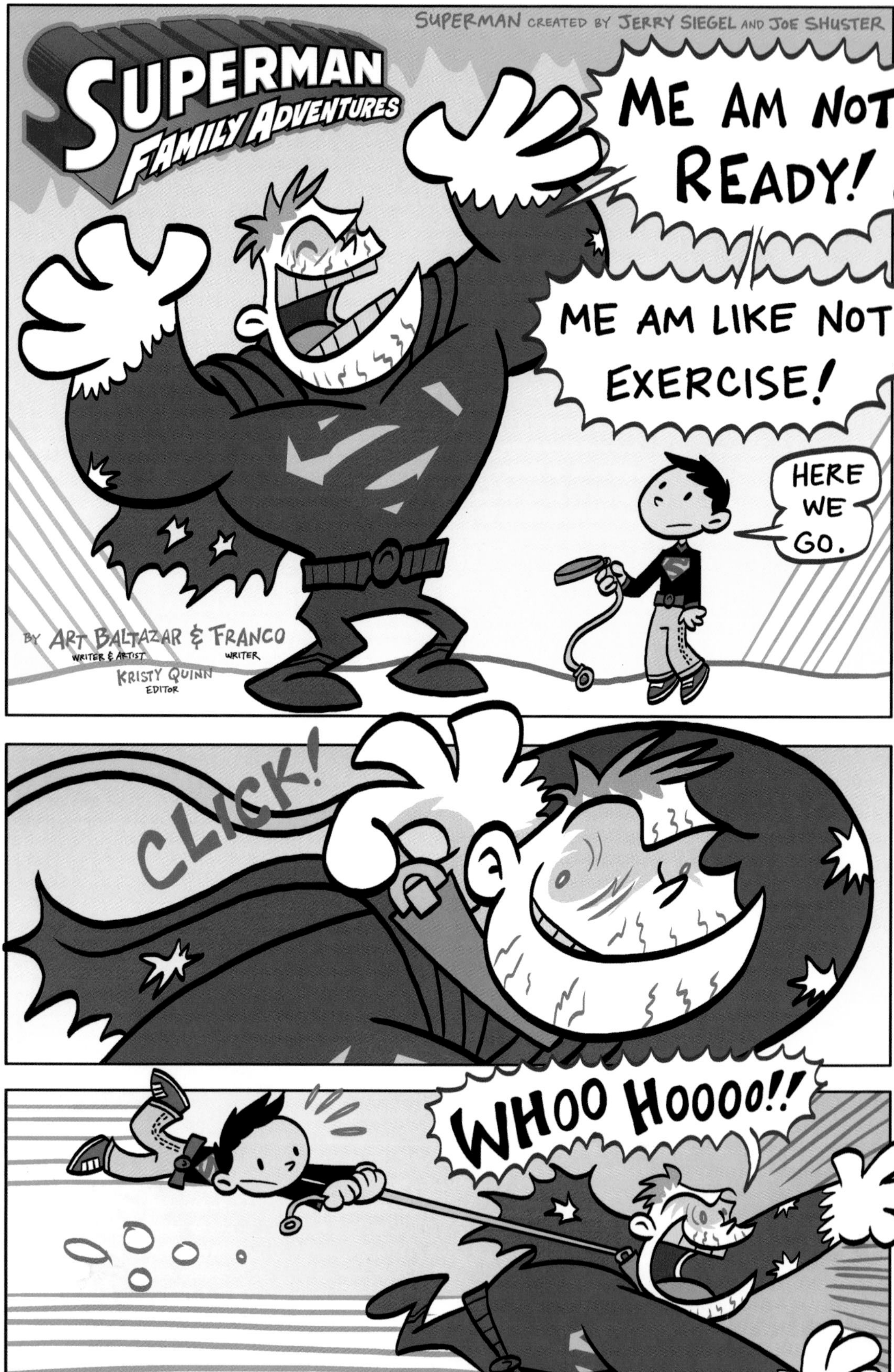
SUPERMAN CREATED BY JERRY SIEGEL AND JOE SHUSTER
SUPERMAN FAMILY ADVENTURES
ME AM NOT READY!
ME AM LIKE NOT EXERCISE!
HERE WE GO.
BY ART BALTAZAR WRITER & ARTIST & FRANCO WRITER
KRISTY QUINN EDITOR
CLICK!
WHOO HOOOO!!

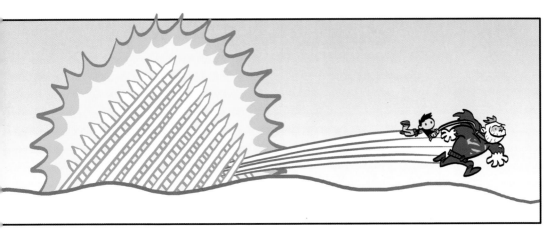

EERT!

WHAT? WHAT IS IT, BIZARRO?

RED?

RED! RED KRYPTONITE! VERY BAD!

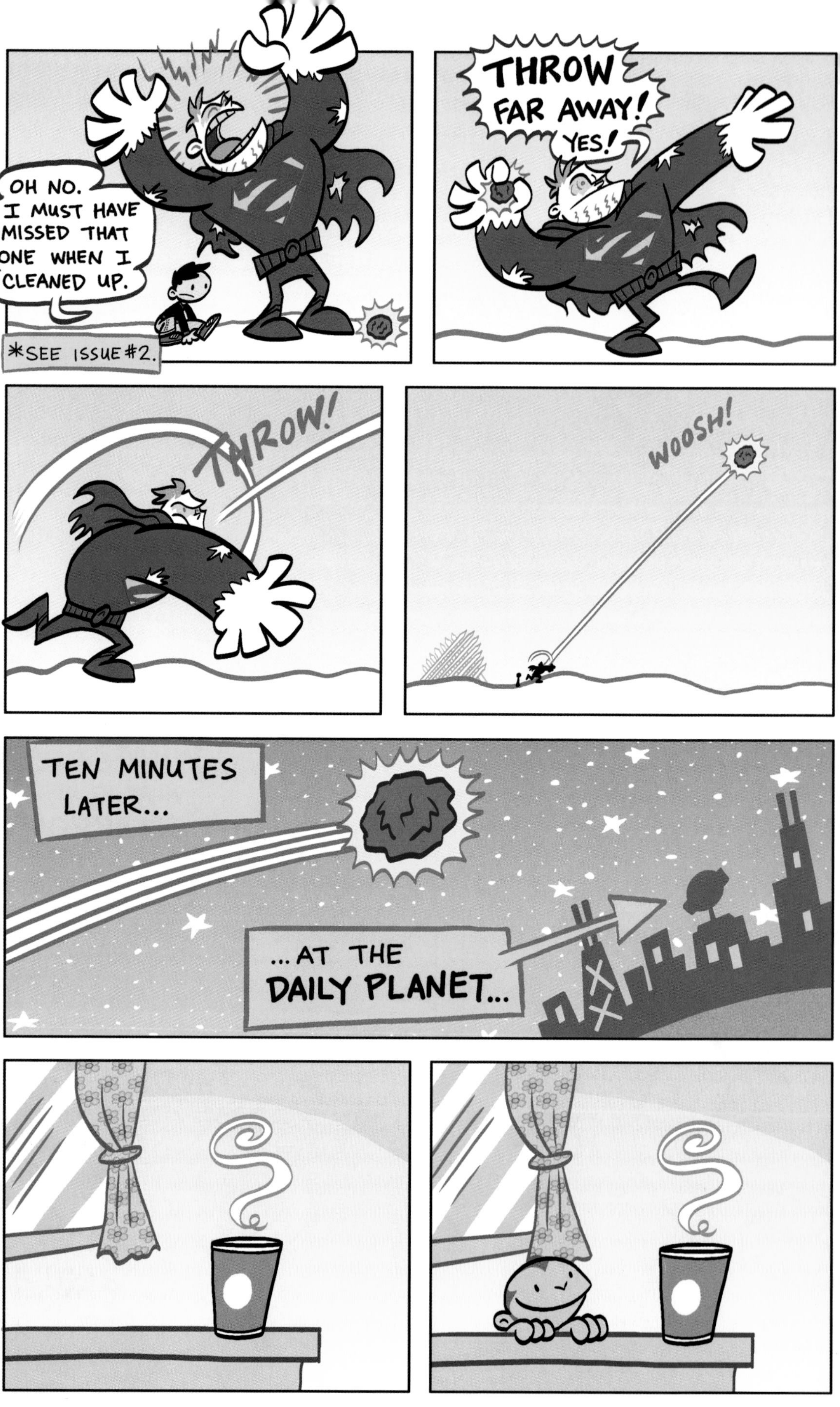

OH NO. I MUST HAVE MISSED THAT ONE WHEN I CLEANED UP.
*SEE ISSUE #2.
THROW FAR AWAY!
YES!
THROW!
WOOSH!
TEN MINUTES LATER...
...AT THE DAILY PLANET...

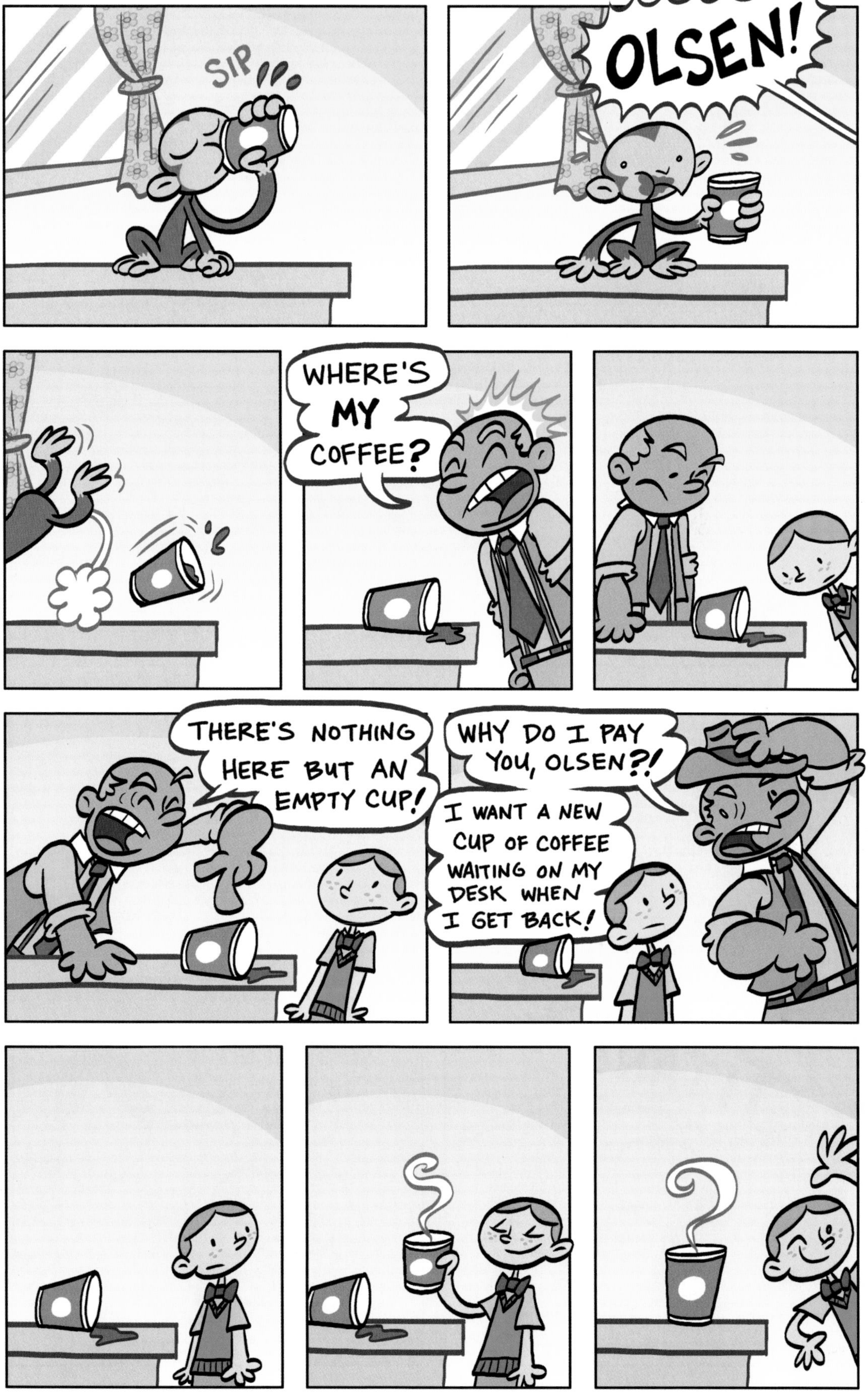
SIP
OLSEN!
WHERE'S MY COFFEE?
THERE'S NOTHING HERE BUT AN EMPTY CUP!
WHY DO I PAY YOU, OLSEN?!
I WANT A NEW CUP OF COFFEE WAITING ON MY DESK WHEN I GET BACK!

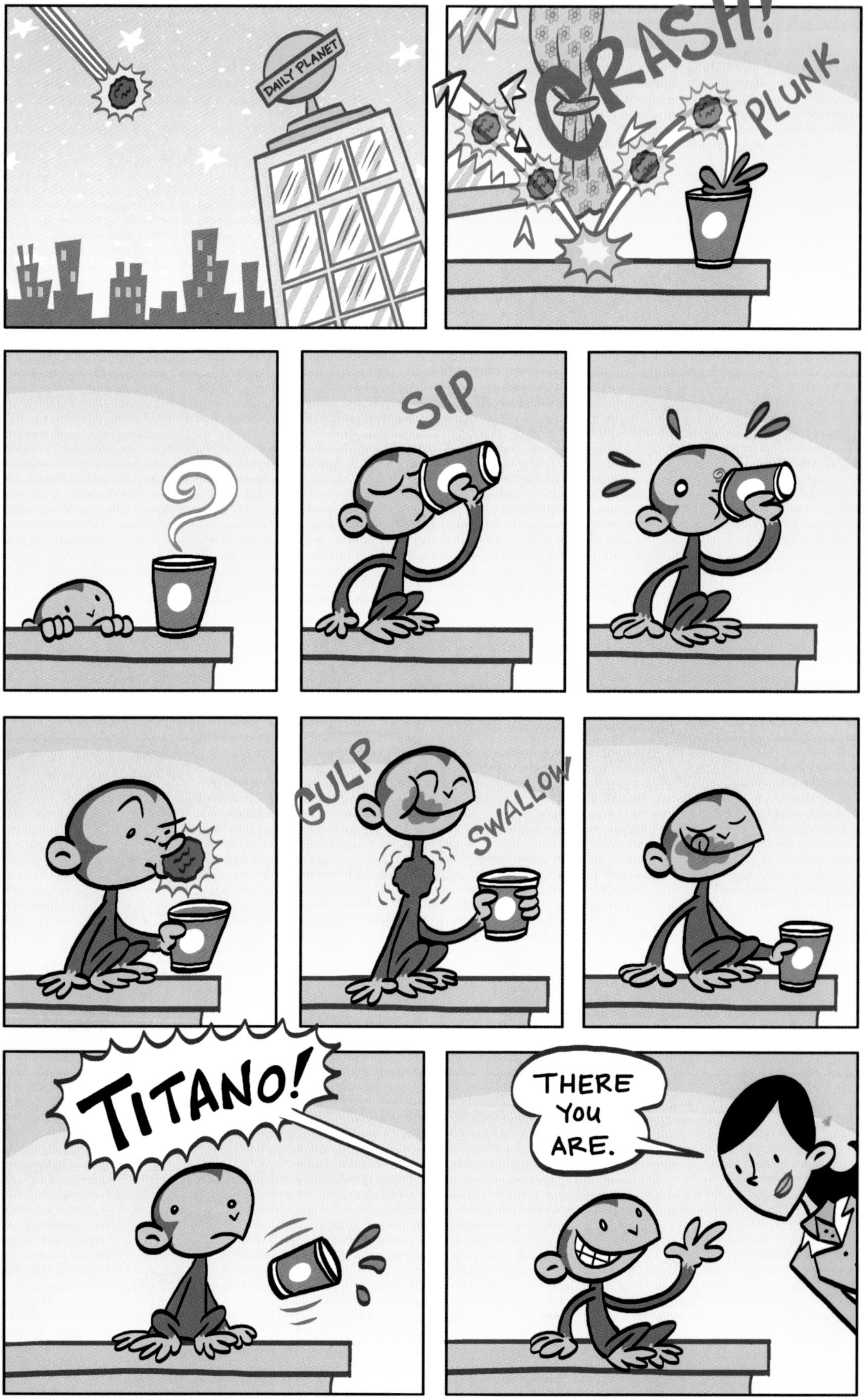

DAILY PLANET
CRASH!
PLUNK
SIP
GULP
SWALLOW
TITANO!
THERE YOU ARE.

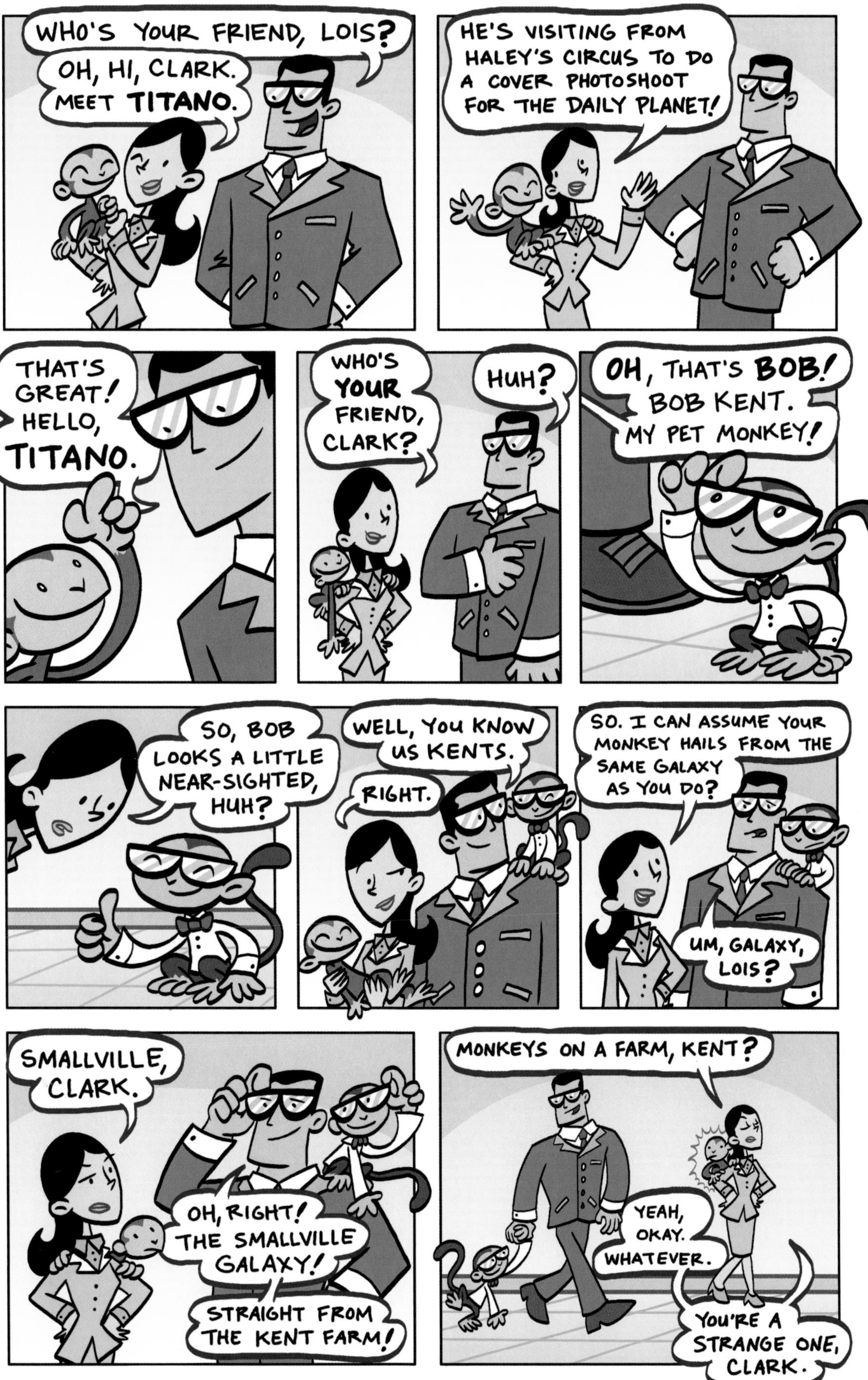
WHO'S YOUR FRIEND, LOIS?
OH, HI, CLARK. MEET TITANO.
HE'S VISITING FROM HALEY'S CIRCUS TO DO A COVER PHOTOSHOOT FOR THE DAILY PLANET!
THAT'S GREAT! HELLO, TITANO.
WHO'S YOUR FRIEND, CLARK?
HUH?
OH, THAT'S BOB! BOB KENT. MY PET MONKEY!
SO, BOB LOOKS A LITTLE NEAR-SIGHTED, HUH?
WELL, YOU KNOW US KENTS.
RIGHT.
SO. I CAN ASSUME YOUR MONKEY HAILS FROM THE SAME GALAXY AS YOU DO?
UM, GALAXY, LOIS?
SMALLVILLE, CLARK.
OH, RIGHT! THE SMALLVILLE GALAXY!
STRAIGHT FROM THE KENT FARM!
MONKEYS ON A FARM, KENT?
YEAH, OKAY. WHATEVER.
YOU'RE A STRANGE ONE, CLARK.

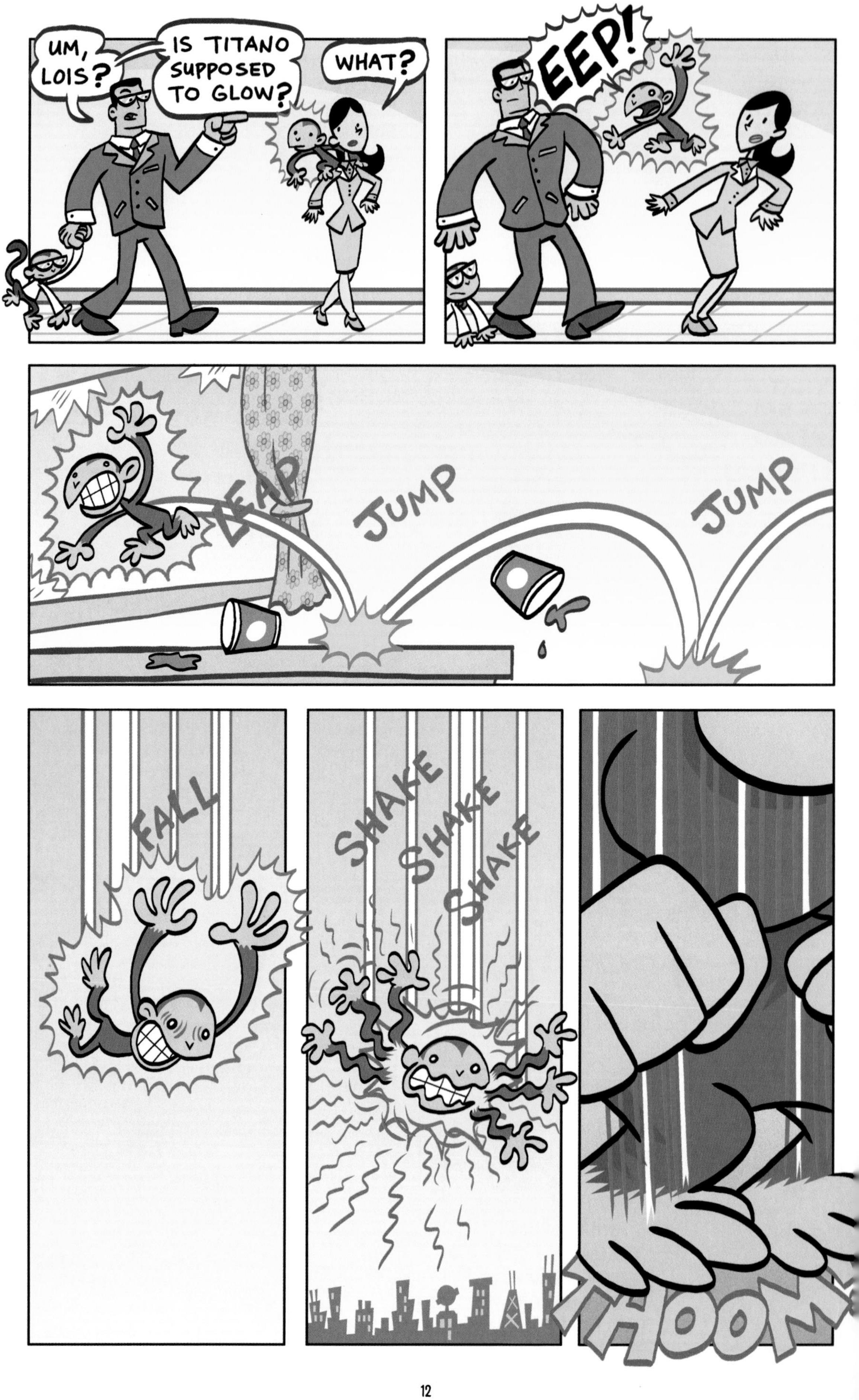
UM, LOIS?
IS TITANO SUPPOSED TO GLOW?
WHAT?
EEP!
LEAP
JUMP
JUMP
FALL
SHAKE
SHAKE
SHAKE
THOOM

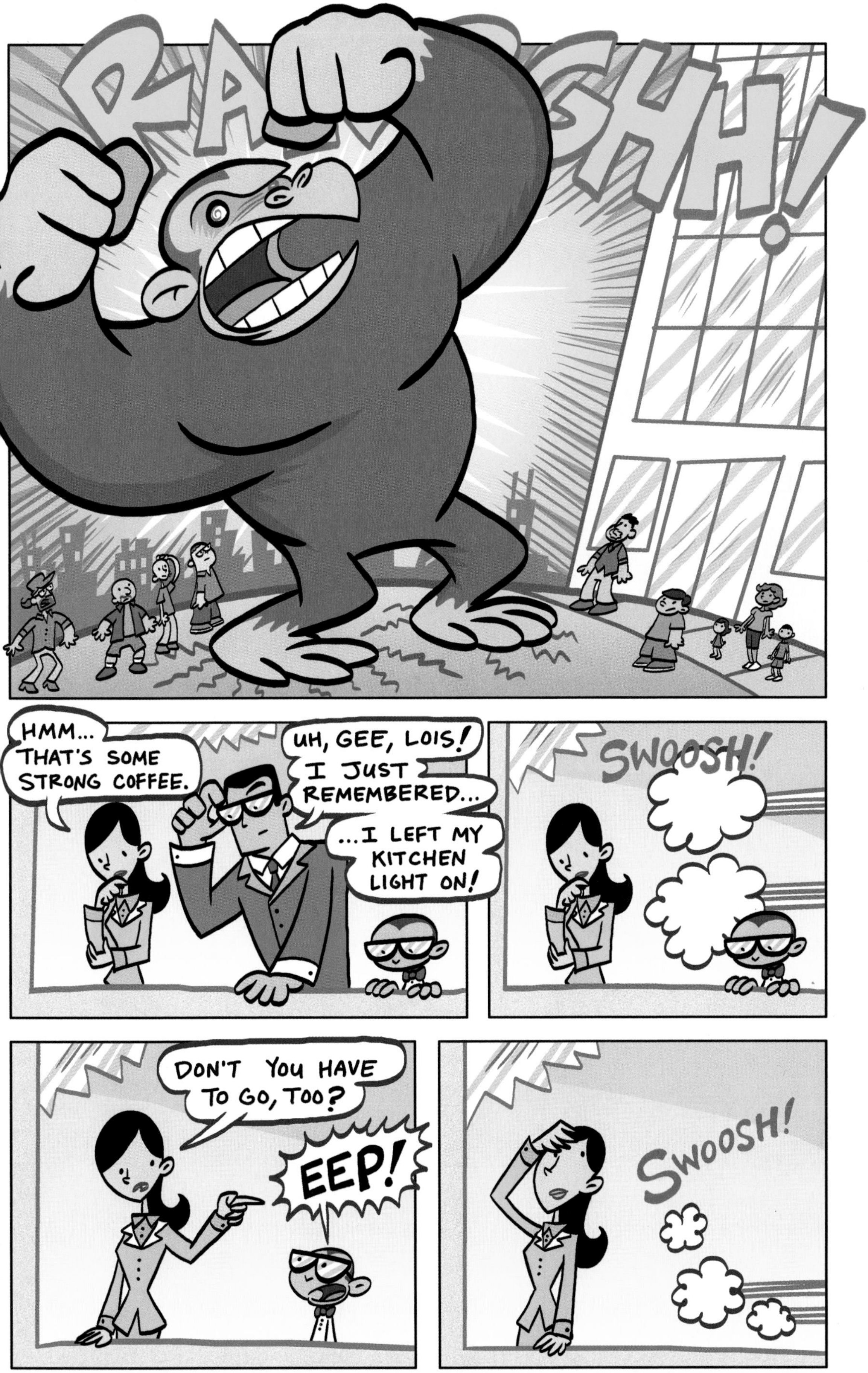
HMM... THAT'S SOME STRONG COFFEE.
UH, GEE, LOIS! I JUST REMEMBERED...
...I LEFT MY KITCHEN LIGHT ON!
SWOOSH!
DON'T YOU HAVE TO GO, TOO?
EEP!
SWOOSH!

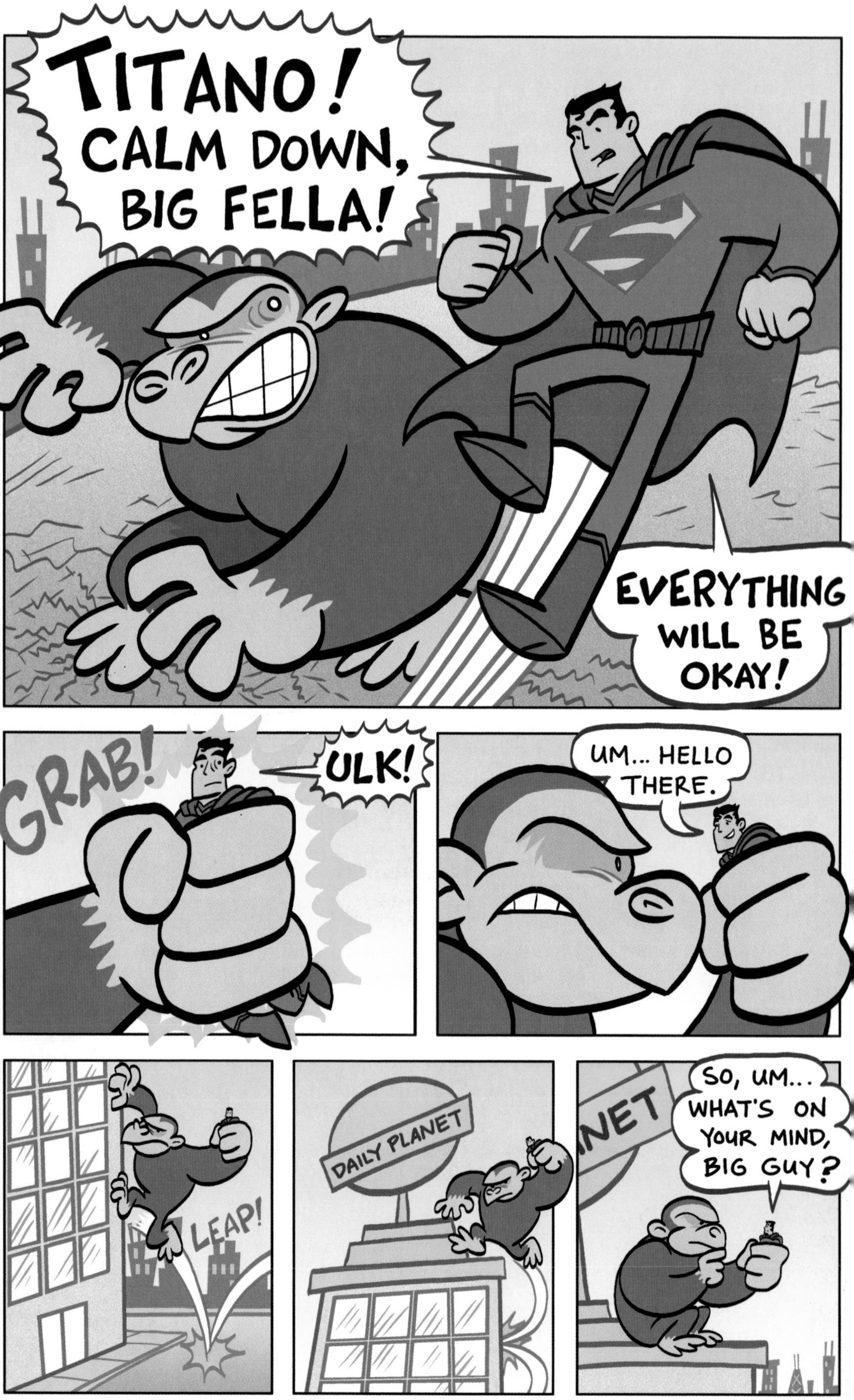
TITANO! CALM DOWN, BIG FELLA!
EVERYTHING WILL BE OKAY!
GRAB!
ULK!
UM... HELLO THERE.
LEAP!
DAILY PLANET
NET
SO, UM... WHAT'S ON YOUR MIND, BIG GUY?

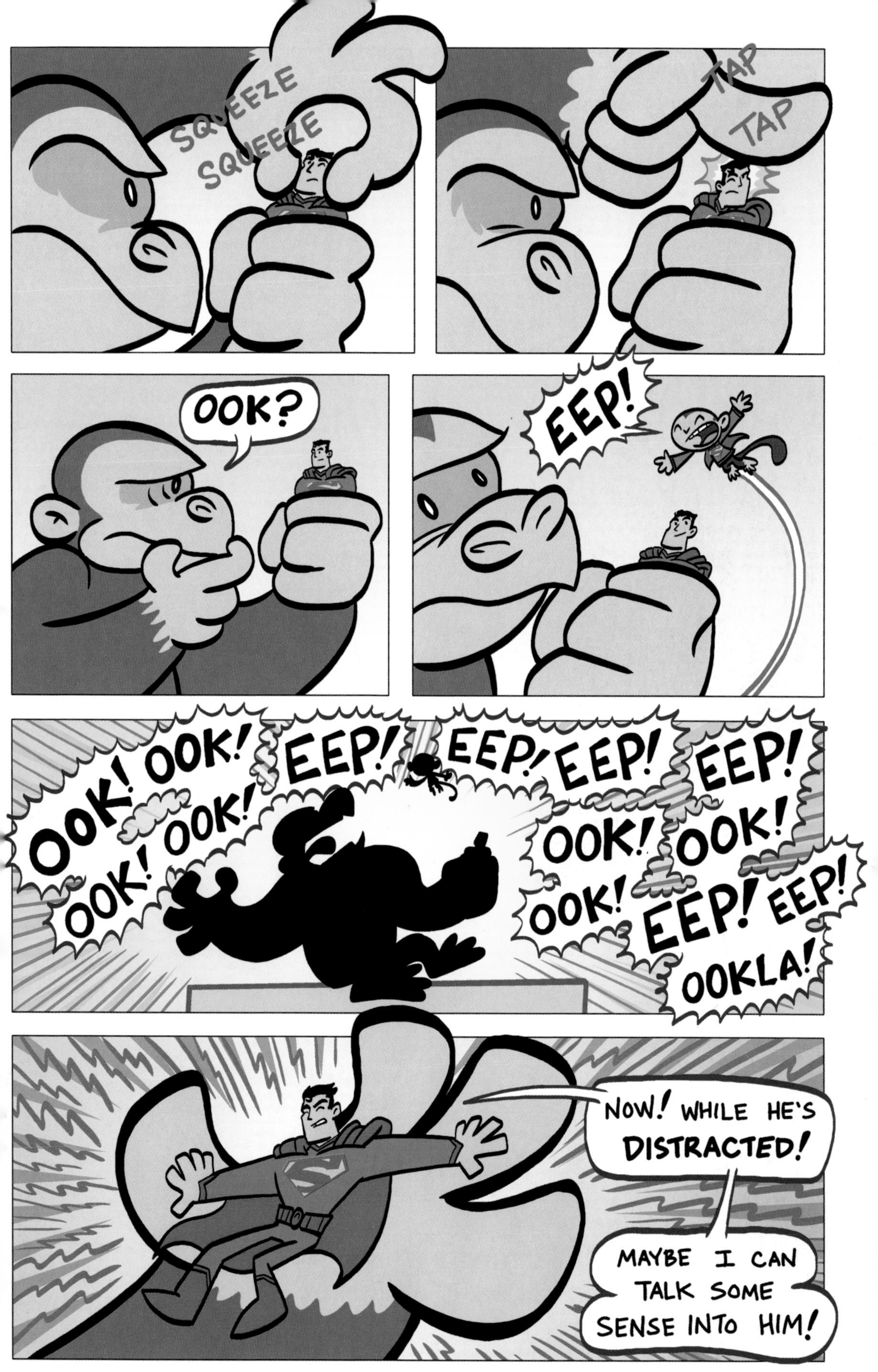
SQUEEZE
SQUEEZE
TAP
TAP
OOK?
EEP!
OOK! OOK!
OOK! OOK!
EEP! EEP! EEP! EEP!
OOK! OOK!
OOK! EEP! EEP!
OOKLA!
NOW! WHILE HE'S DISTRACTED!
MAYBE I CAN TALK SOME SENSE INTO HIM!

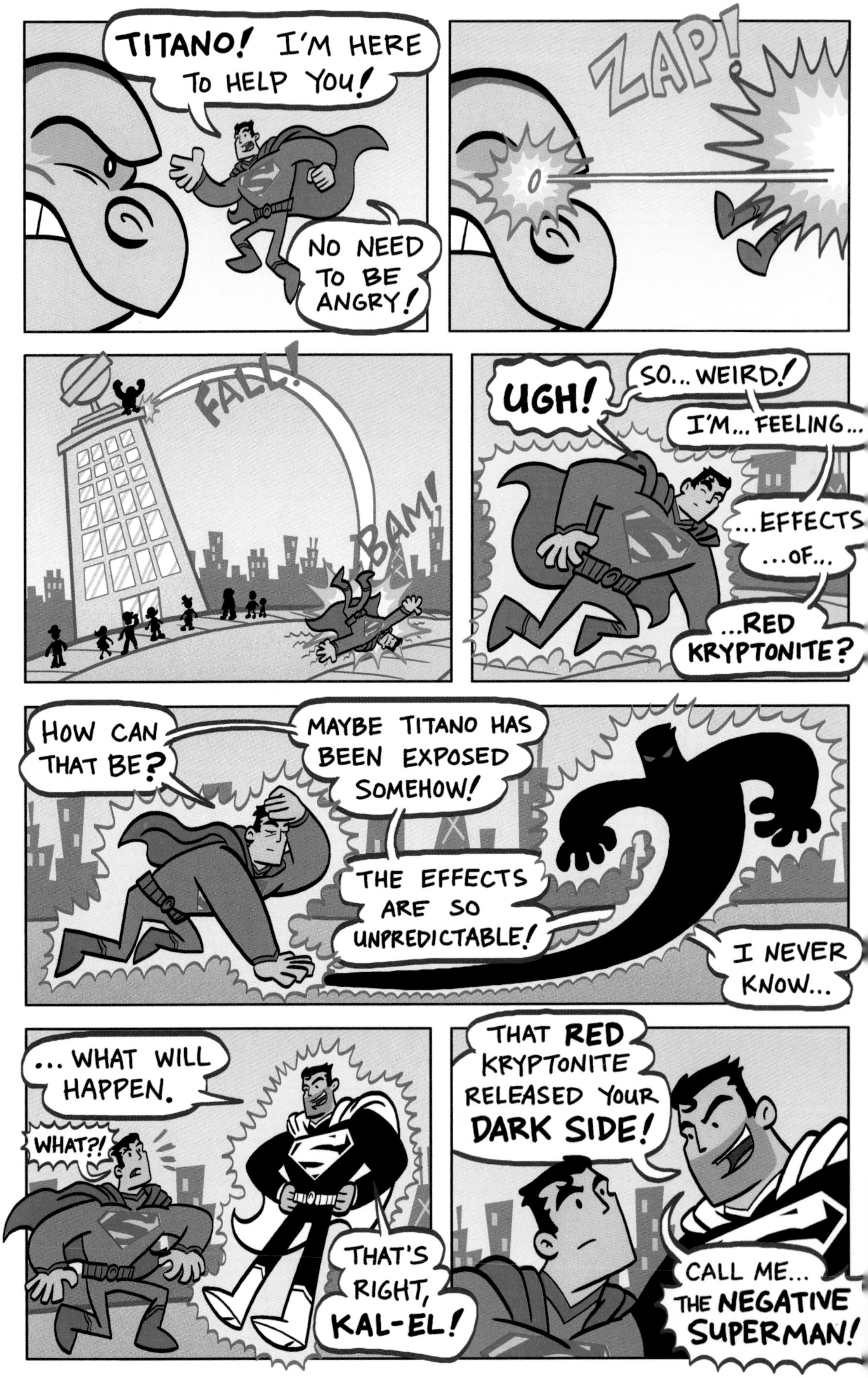

TITANO! I'M HERE TO HELP YOU!
NO NEED TO BE ANGRY!
ZAP!
FALL!
BAM!
UGH!
SO... WEIRD!
I'M... FEELING...
...EFFECTS ...OF...
...RED KRYPTONITE?
HOW CAN THAT BE?
MAYBE TITANO HAS BEEN EXPOSED SOMEHOW!
THE EFFECTS ARE SO UNPREDICTABLE!
I NEVER KNOW...
... WHAT WILL HAPPEN.
WHAT?!
THAT'S RIGHT, KAL-EL!
THAT RED KRYPTONITE RELEASED YOUR DARK SIDE!
CALL ME... THE NEGATIVE SUPERMAN!

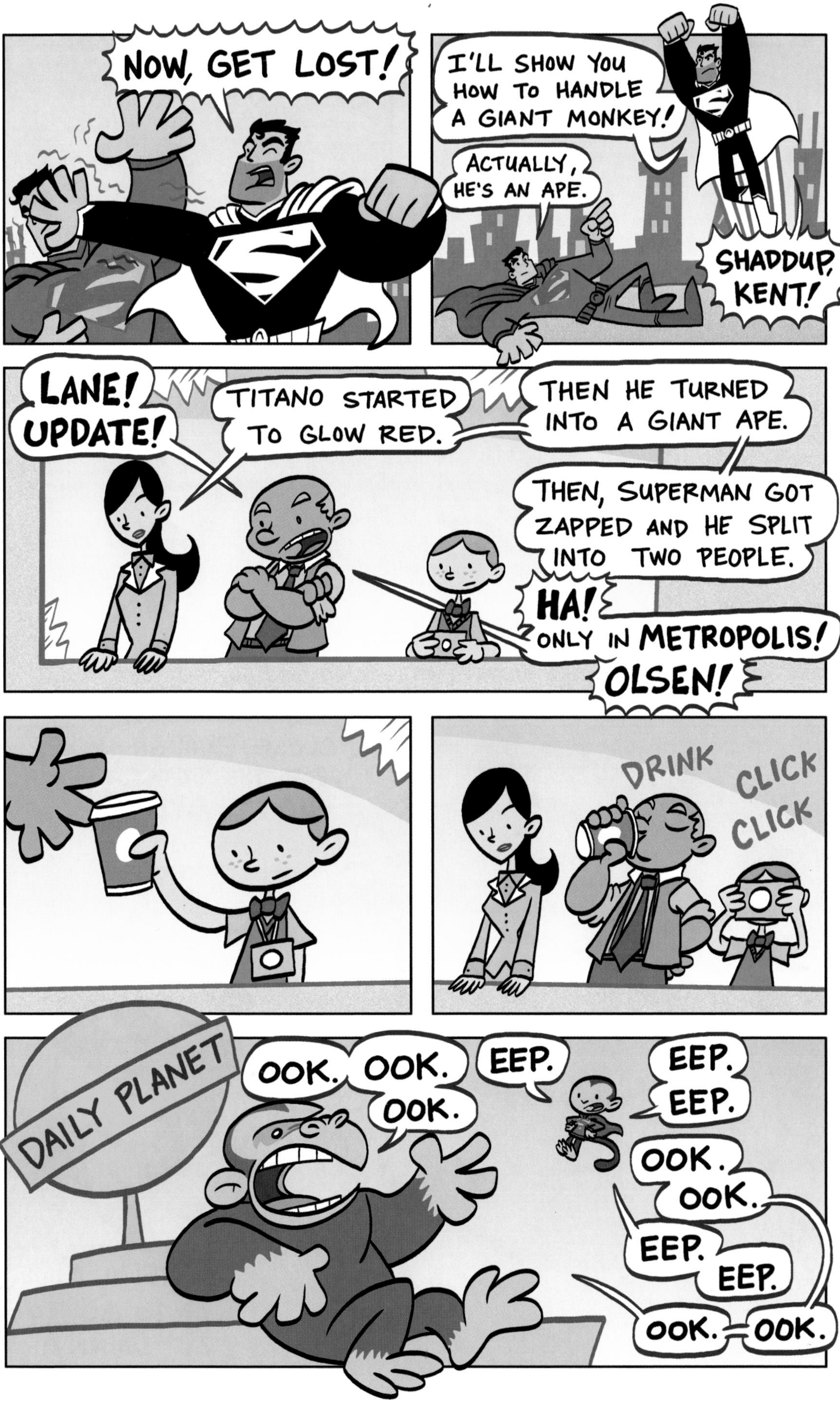
NOW, GET LOST!
I'LL SHOW YOU HOW TO HANDLE A GIANT MONKEY!
ACTUALLY, HE'S AN APE.
SHADDUP, KENT!
LANE! UPDATE!
TITANO STARTED TO GLOW RED.
THEN HE TURNED INTO A GIANT APE.
THEN, SUPERMAN GOT ZAPPED AND HE SPLIT INTO TWO PEOPLE.
HA! ONLY IN METROPOLIS!
OLSEN!
DRINK
CLICK CLICK
DAILY PLANET
OOK. OOK. OOK.
EEP.
EEP. EEP.
OOK. OOK.
EEP. EEP.
OOK. OOK.

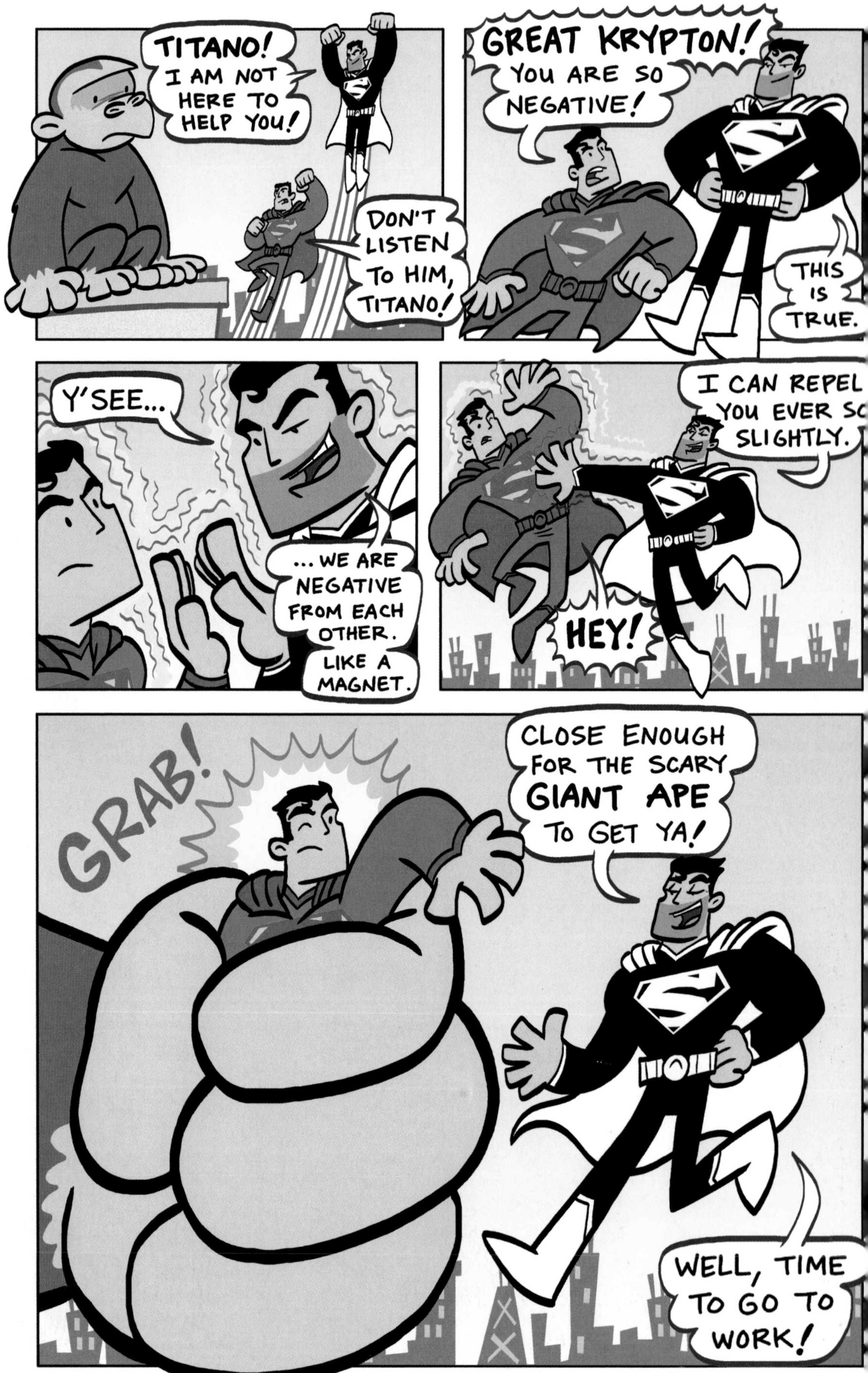
TITANO! I AM NOT HERE TO HELP YOU!
DON'T LISTEN TO HIM, TITANO!
GREAT KRYPTON! YOU ARE SO NEGATIVE!
THIS IS TRUE.
Y'SEE...
... WE ARE NEGATIVE FROM EACH OTHER.
LIKE A MAGNET.
I CAN REPEL YOU EVER SO SLIGHTLY.
HEY!
GRAB!
CLOSE ENOUGH FOR THE SCARY GIANT APE TO GET YA!
WELL, TIME TO GO TO WORK!

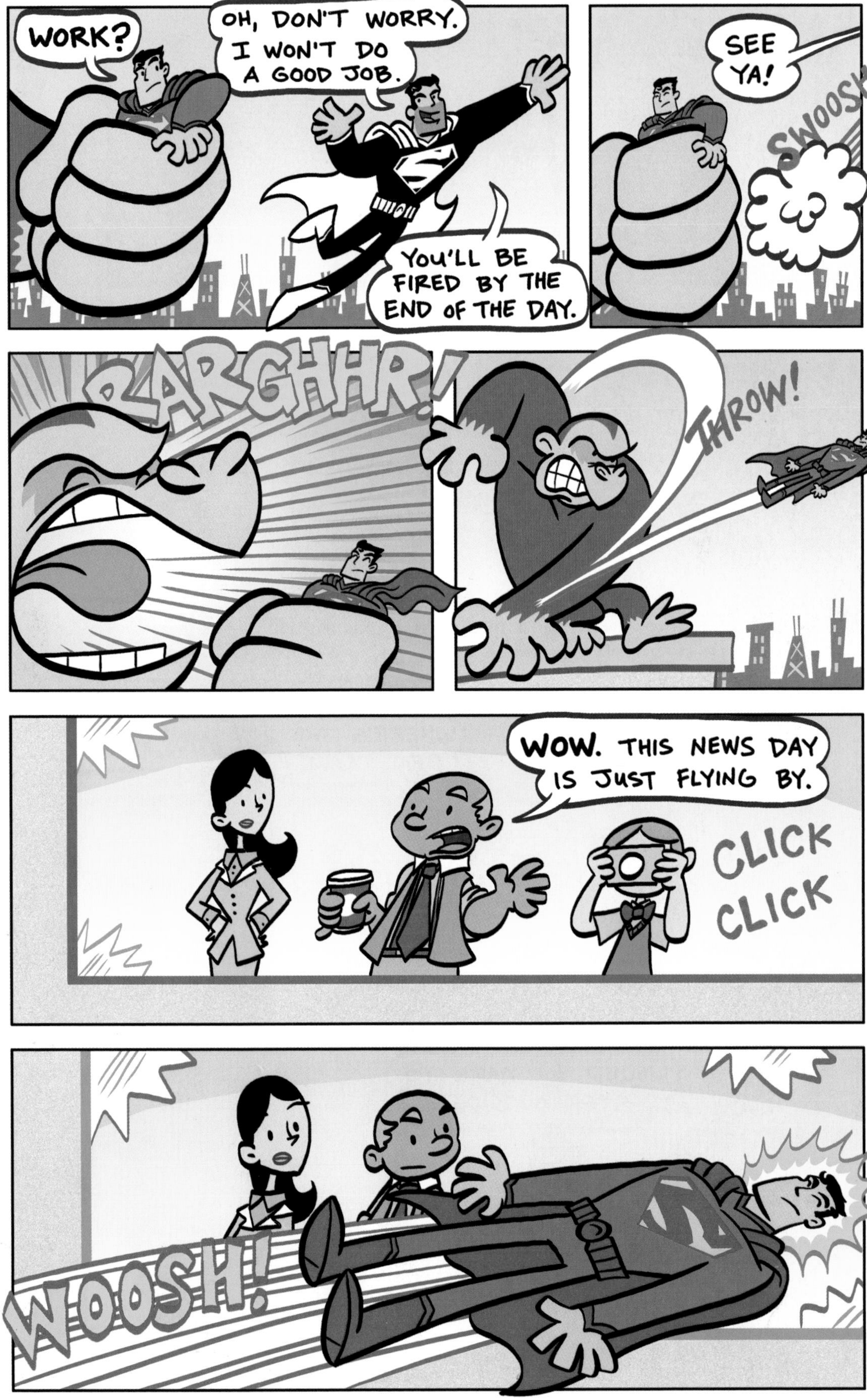

WORK?
OH, DON'T WORRY. I WON'T DO A GOOD JOB.
YOU'LL BE FIRED BY THE END OF THE DAY.
SEE YA!
SWOOSH
RARGHHR!
THROW!
WOW. THIS NEWS DAY IS JUST FLYING BY.
CLICK CLICK
WOOSH!

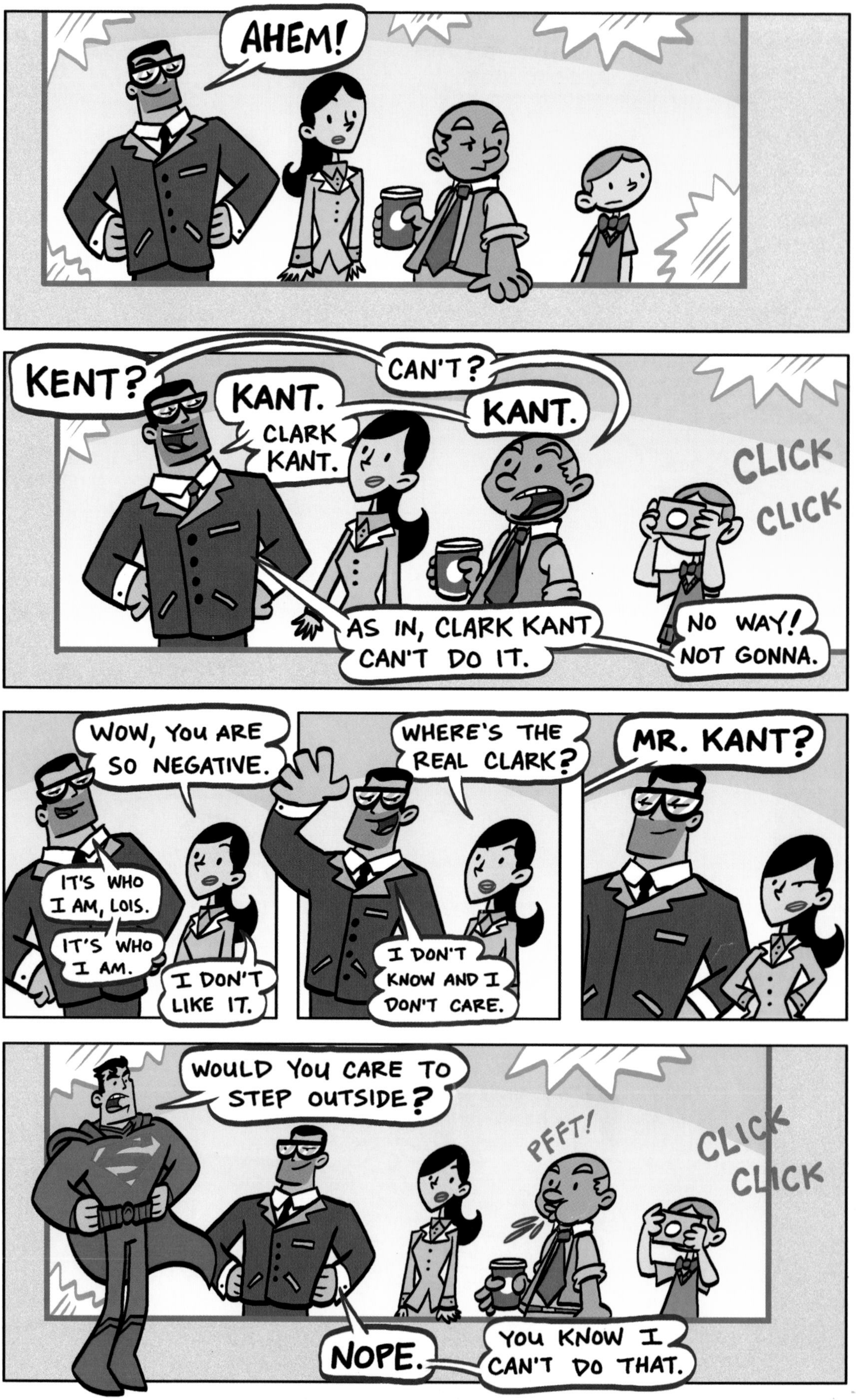
AHEM!
KENT?
CAN'T?
KANT.
CLARK KANT.
KANT.
CLICK CLICK
AS IN, CLARK KANT CAN'T DO IT.
NO WAY! NOT GONNA.
WOW, YOU ARE SO NEGATIVE.
IT'S WHO I AM, LOIS.
IT'S WHO I AM.
I DON'T LIKE IT.
WHERE'S THE REAL CLARK?
I DON'T KNOW AND I DON'T CARE.
MR. KANT?
WOULD YOU CARE TO STEP OUTSIDE?
PFFT!
CLICK CLICK
NOPE.
YOU KNOW I CAN'T DO THAT.

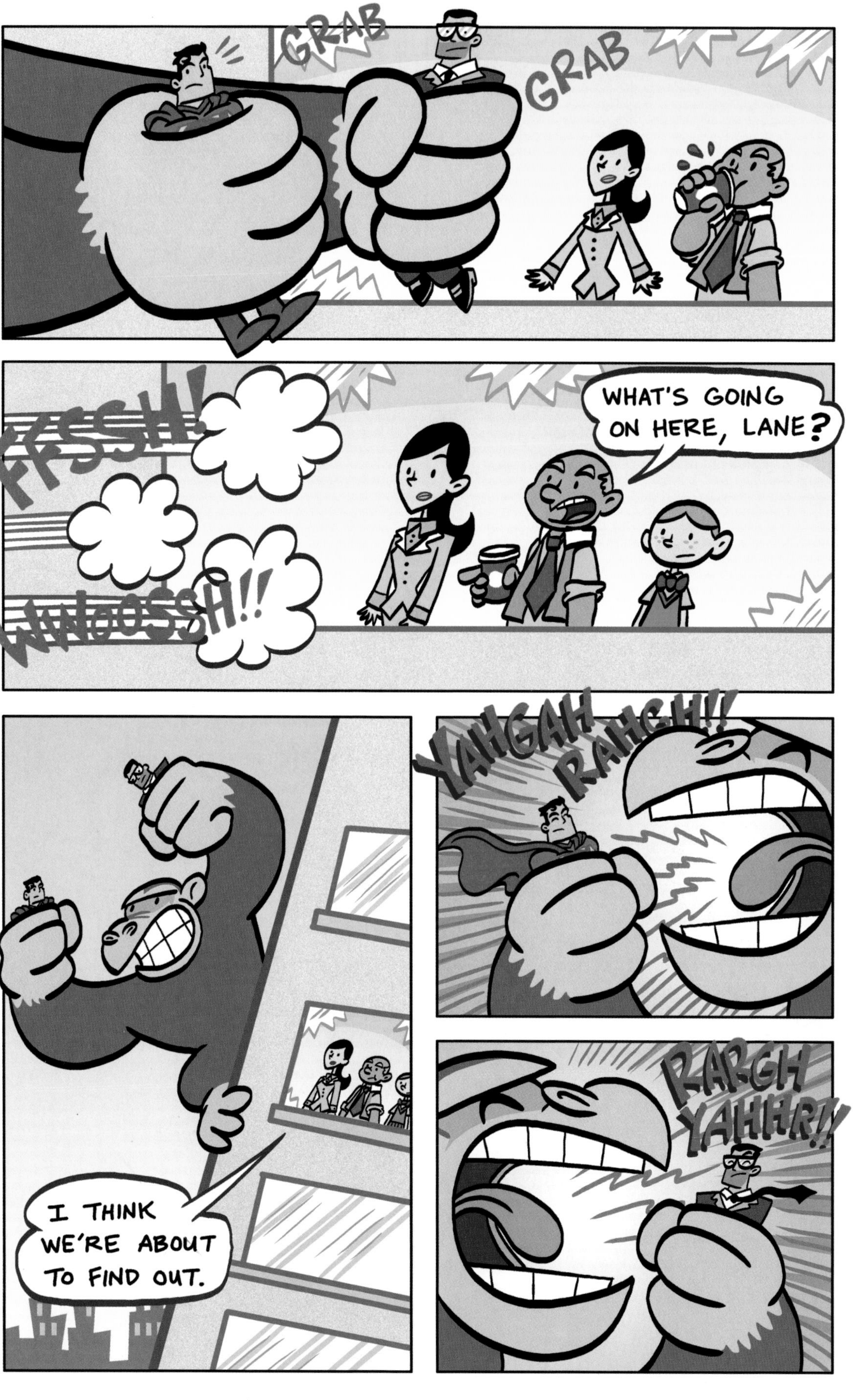
GRAB
GRAB
FFSSH!
WHOOSSH!!
WHAT'S GOING ON HERE, LANE?
I THINK WE'RE ABOUT TO FIND OUT.
YAHGAH RAHGH!!
RARGH YAHHR!!

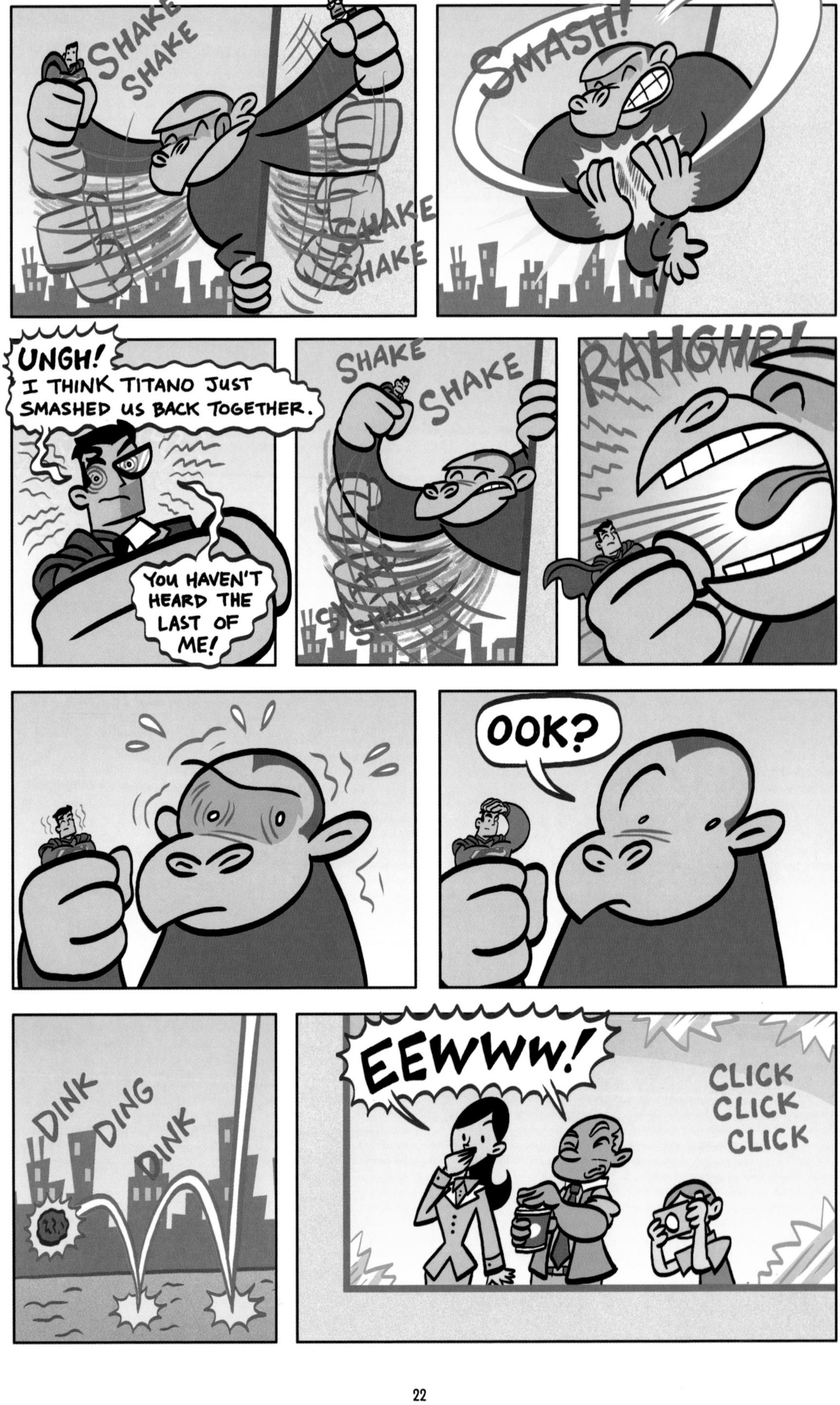
SHAKE
SHAKE
SHAKE
SHAKE
SMASH!
UNGH!
I THINK TITANO JUST SMASHED US BACK TOGETHER.
YOU HAVEN'T HEARD THE LAST OF ME!
SHAKE
SHAKE
RAHGHR!
OOK?
DINK
DING
DINK
EEWWW!
CLICK
CLICK
CLICK

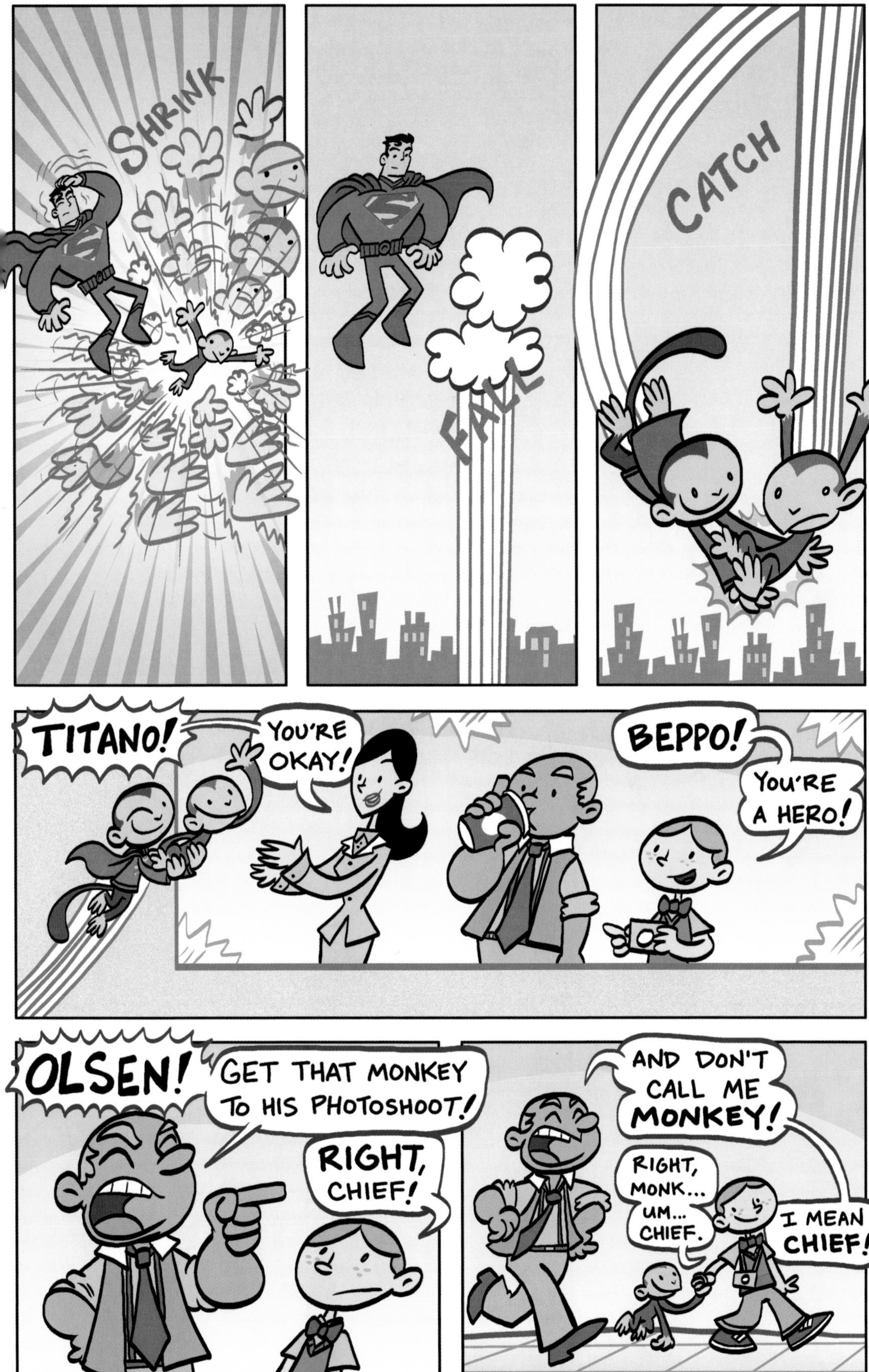
SHRINK
FALL
CATCH
TITANO!
YOU'RE OKAY!
BEPPO!
YOU'RE A HERO!
OLSEN!
GET THAT MONKEY TO HIS PHOTOSHOOT!
RIGHT, CHIEF!
AND DON'T CALL ME MONKEY!
RIGHT, MONK... UM... CHIEF.
I MEAN CHIEF!

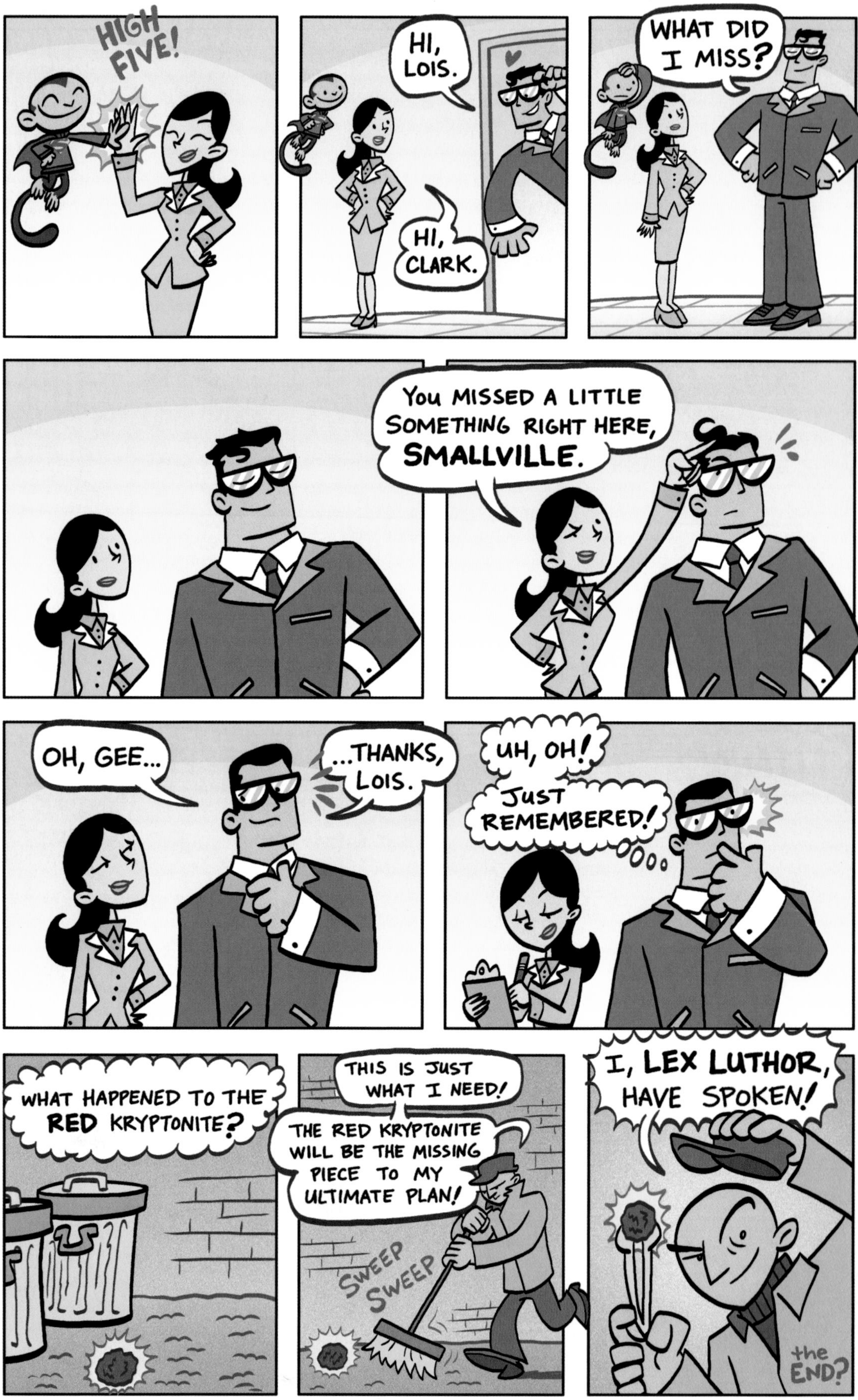
HIGH FIVE!
HI, LOIS.
HI, CLARK.
WHAT DID I MISS?
You MISSED A LITTLE SOMETHING RIGHT HERE, SMALLVILLE.
OH, GEE...
...THANKS, LOIS.
UH, OH!
JUST REMEMBERED!
WHAT HAPPENED TO THE RED KRYPTONITE?
THIS IS JUST WHAT I NEED!
THE RED KRYPTONITE WILL BE THE MISSING PIECE TO MY ULTIMATE PLAN!
SWEEP SWEEP
I, LEX LUTHOR, HAVE SPOKEN!
the END?

-HE'S BACK?! WHAT DOES THIS MEAN? ONLY TIME WILL TELL!

SUPERMAN®
FAMILY ADVENTURES™

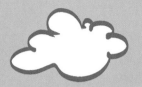

CREATORS

ART BALTAZAR IS A CARTOONIST MACHINE FROM THE HEART OF CHICAGO! HE DEFINES CARTOONS AND COMICS NOT ONLY AS AN ART STYLE, BUT AS A WAY OF LIFE. CURRENTLY, ART IS THE CREATIVE FORCE BEHIND THE NEW YORK TIMES BEST-SELLING, EISNER AWARD-WINNING, DC COMICS SERIES TINY TITANS, AND THE CO-WRITER FOR BILLY BATSON AND THE MAGIC OF SHAZAM! AND CO-CREATOR OF SUPERMAN FAMILY ADVENTURES. ART IS LIVING THE DREAM! HE DRAWS COMICS AND NEVER HAS TO LEAVE THE HOUSE. HE LIVES WITH HIS LOVELY WIFE, ROSE, BIG BOY SONNY, LITTLE BOY GORDON, AND LITTLE GIRL AUDREY. RIGHT ON!

ART BALTAZAR

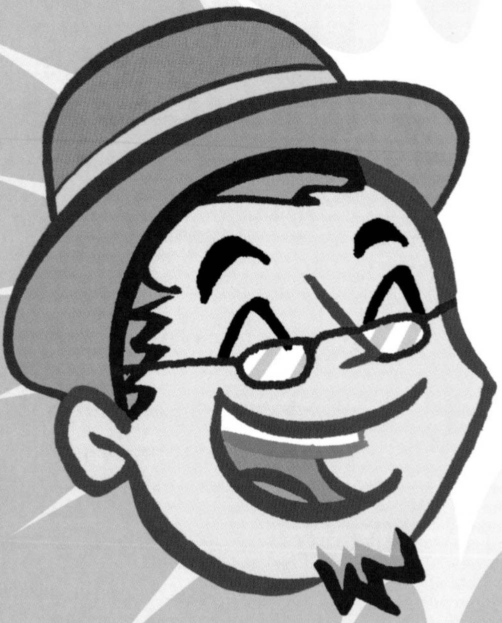

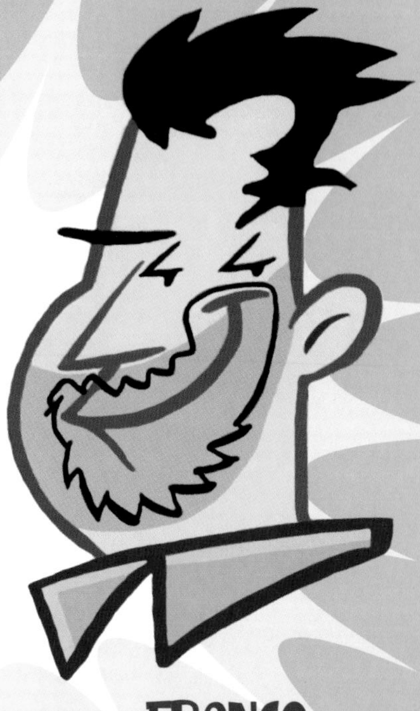

FRANCO

FRANCO AURELIANI, BRONX, NEW YORK BORN WRITER AND ARTIST, HAS BEEN DRAWING COMICS SINCE HE COULD HOLD A CRAYON. CURRENTLY RESIDING IN UPSTATE NEW YORK WITH HIS WIFE, IVETTE, AND SON, NICOLAS, FRANCO SPENDS MOST OF HIS DAYS IN A BATCAVE-LIKE STUDIO WHERE HE PRODUCES DC'S TINY TITANS COMICS. IN 1995, FRANCO FOUNDED BLINDWOLF STUDIOS, AN INDEPENDENT ART STUDIO WHERE HE AND FELLOW CREATORS CAN CREATE CHILDREN'S COMICS. FRANCO IS THE CREATOR, ARTIST, AND WRITER OF WEIRDSVILLE, L'IL CREEPS, AND EAGLE ALL STAR, AS WELL AS THE CO-CREATOR AND WRITER OF PATRICK THE WOLF BOY. WHEN HE'S NOT WRITING AND DRAWING, FRANCO ALSO TEACHES HIGH SCHOOL ART.

GLOSSARY

backtrack (BAK-trak)– to go back over a course or path (Or to reverse a position or stand)

collision (kuh-LIZH-uhn)–the act or instance of crashing together forcefully, often at high speeds

distracted (diss-TRAK-tuhd)–had the attention or mind on something else

fortress (FOR-triss)–a place that is strengthened against attack

galaxy (GAL-uhk-see)–a very large group of stars and planets

hails (HAYLZ)–to come from

magnet (MAG-nit)–a piece of metal that attracts iron or steel

meteorite (MEE-tee-ur-rite)–a remaining part of a meteor that falls to Earth before it has burned up

near-sighted (NEER-site-uhd)–able to see near things more clearly than distant ones

negative (NEG-uh-tiv)–not thinking positively or being helpful

solitude (SOL-uh-tood)–the quality or state of being alone or far-off from society

ultimate (UHL-tuh-mit)–greatest or best

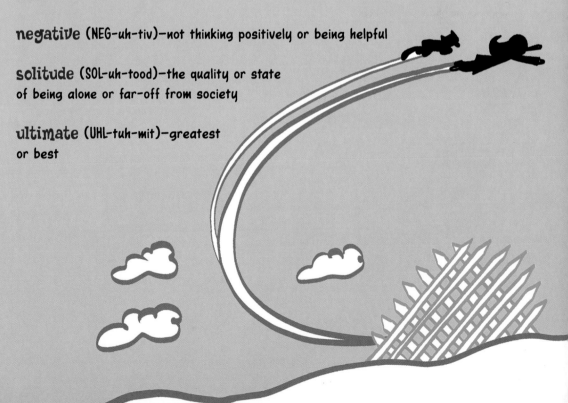

VISUAL QUESTIONS & PROMPTS

1. THE RED KRYPTONITE CREATES A NEGATIVE VERSION OF SUPERMAN. GO BACK THROUGH THE STORY AND FIND AT LEAST TWO THINGS THAT MAKE HIM DIFFERENT FROM THE MAN OF STEEL.

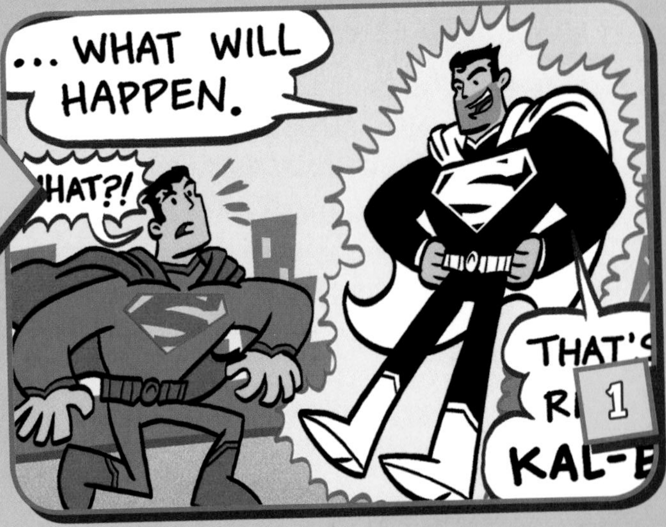

... WHAT WILL HAPPEN.
HAT?!
THAT'S
R
KAL-E
1

2. AT THE END OF THE STORY, LEX LUTHOR FINDS THE CHUNK OF RED KRYPTONITE. WHAT DO YOU THINK HE PLANS TO DO WITH IT? WRITE A FEW PARAGRAPHS ABOUT THE VILLAIN'S EVIL PLAN.

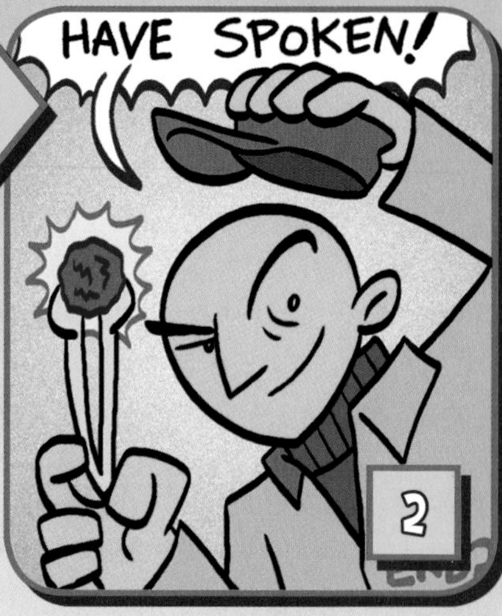

HAVE SPOKEN!
2

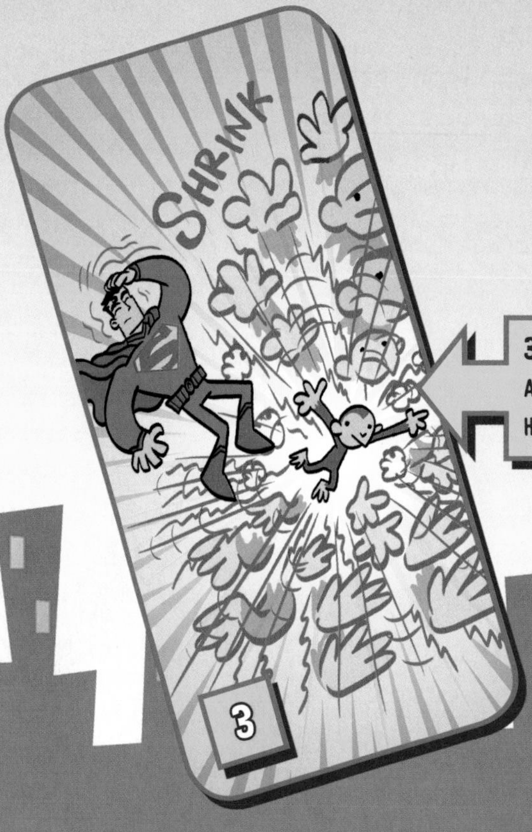

SHRINK
3

3. WHAT IS HAPPENING IN THE PANEL AT LEFT, FROM PAGE 23. EXPLAIN HOW YOU GOT YOUR ANSWER.

4. ON PAGE 10, TITANO SWALLOWS THE CHUNK OF RED KRYPTONITE. HOW DOES THE APE FINALLY GET RID OF IT? EXPLAIN.

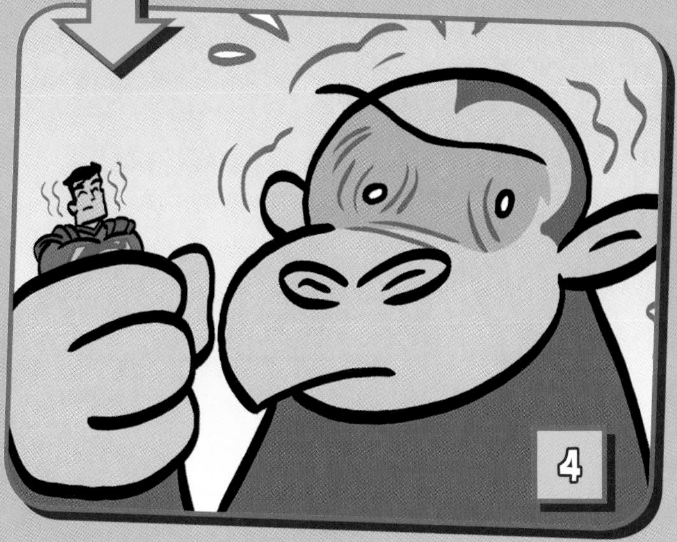

5. IN COMIC BOOKS, SOUND EFFECTS (ALSO KNOWN AS SFX) ARE USED TO SHOW SOUNDS. MAKE A LIST OF ALL THE SOUND EFFECTS IN THIS BOOK, AND THEN WRITE A DEFINITION FOR EACH TERM. SOON, YOU'LL HAVE YOUR OWN SFX DICTIONARY!

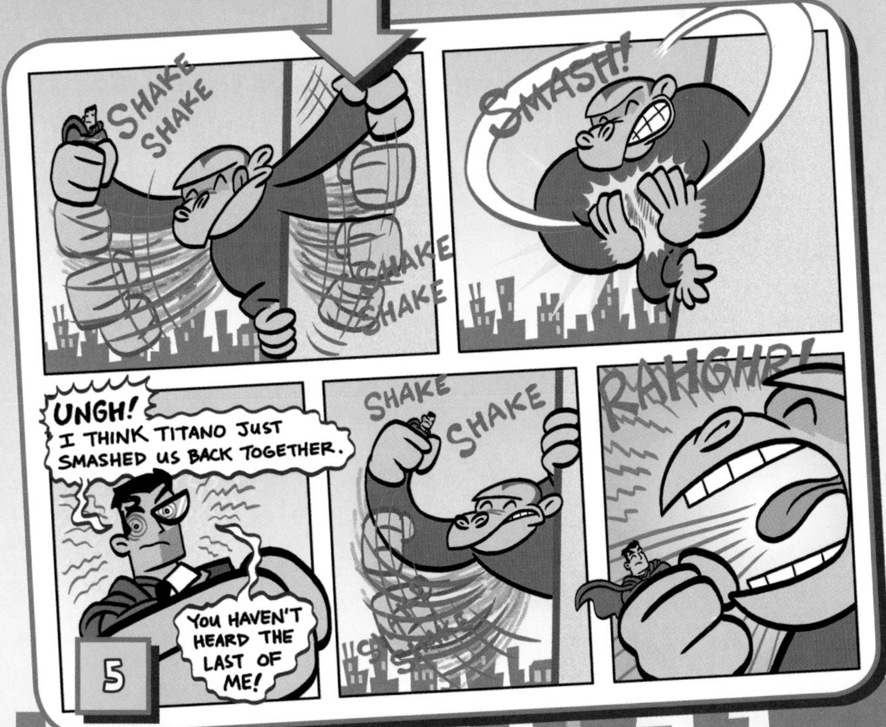

SHAKE
SHAKE
SHAKE
SHAKE
SMASH!
UNGH!
I THINK TITANO JUST SMASHED US BACK TOGETHER.
YOU HAVEN'T HEARD THE LAST OF ME!
5
SHAKE
SHAKE
RAHGHR!

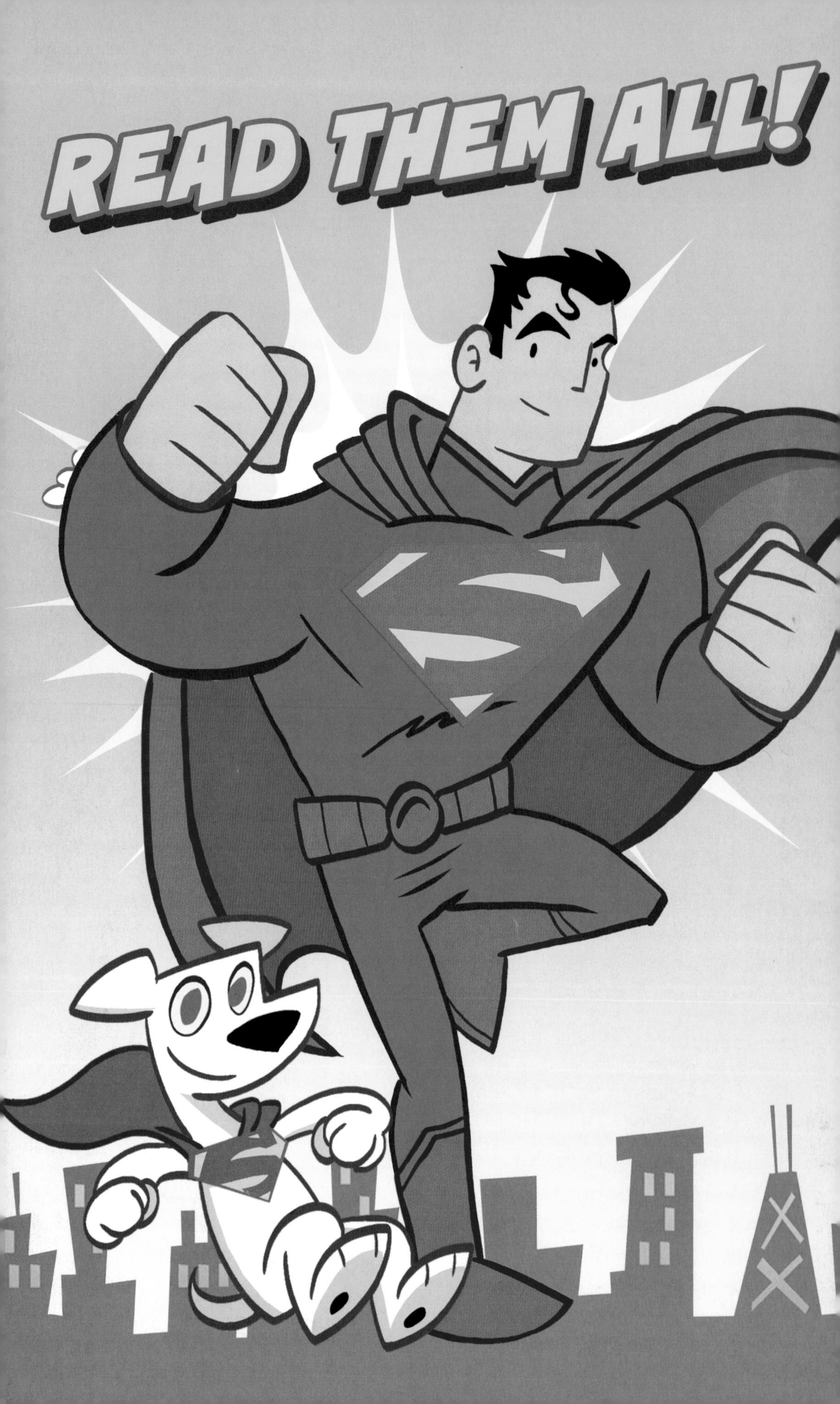
READ THEM ALL!

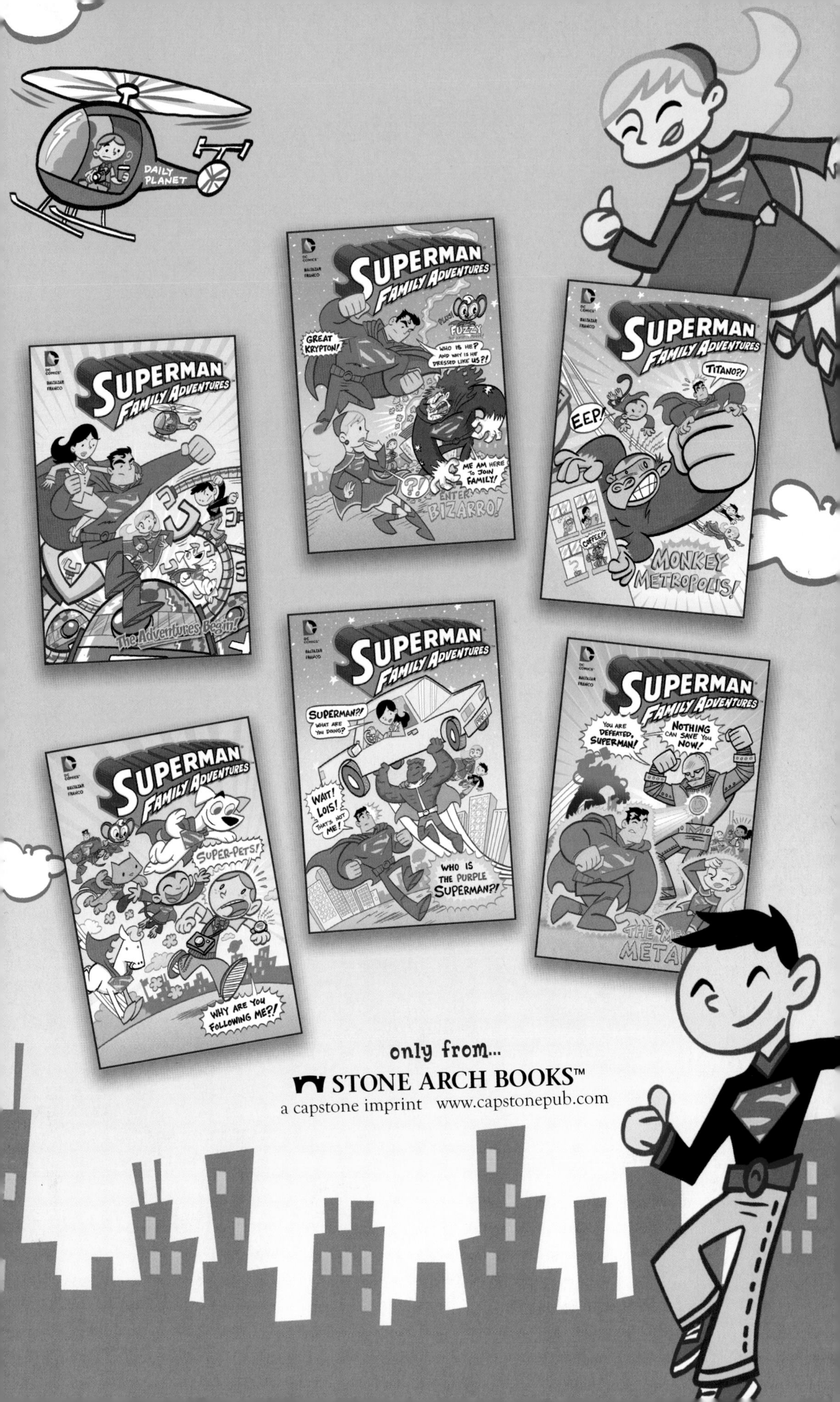
DAILY PLANET
DC COMICS
BALTAZAR FRANCO
SUPERMAN FAMILY ADVENTURES
The Adventures Begin!
GREAT KRYPTON!
PLUS! FUZZY
WHO IS HE? AND WHY IS HE DRESSED LIKE US?!
ME AM HERE TO JOIN FAMILY!
?!
ENTER BIZARRO!
TITANO?!
EEP!
COFFEE!?
MONKEY METROPOLIS!
SUPER-PETS!
WHY ARE YOU FOLLOWING ME?!
SUPERMAN?! WHAT ARE YOU DOING?
WAIT! LOIS! THAT'S NOT ME!
WHO IS THE PURPLE SUPERMAN?!
YOU ARE DEFEATED, SUPERMAN!
NOTHING CAN SAVE YOU NOW!
only from...
STONE ARCH BOOKS™
a capstone imprint www.capstonepub.com

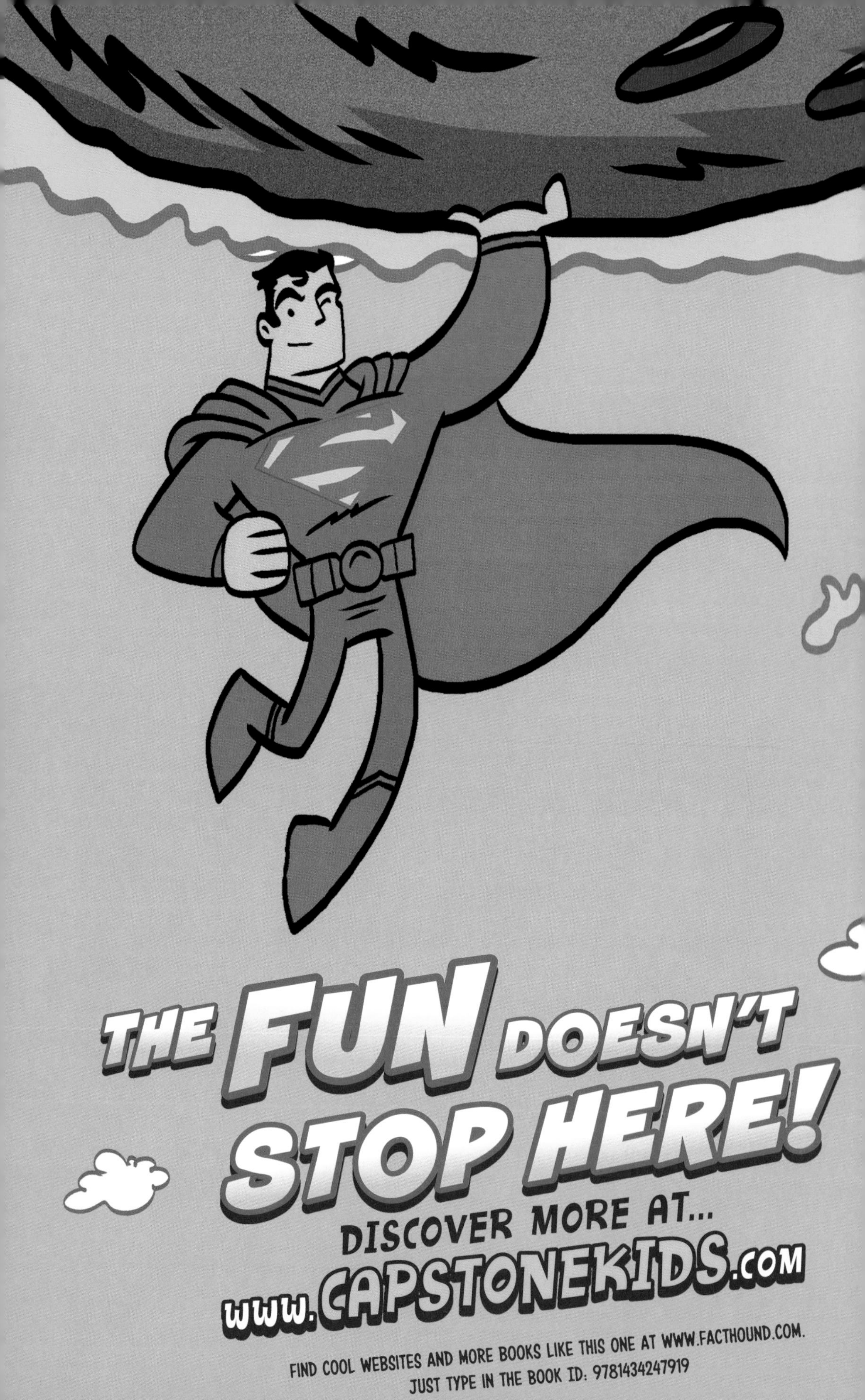